BACKYARDS HAVE BODIES

A SADIE MCINTYRE MYSTERY

BARBARA WALLACE

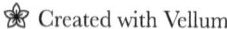

ALSO BY BARBARA WALLACE

The Sadie McIntyre Mystery Series
The Suburbs Have Secrets

This is for Peter. Thank you for 31 years of patience, love, and commitment.

1

_____

"Explain to me again why a truck leaving downtown Boston is a reason to throw a party?" I asked.

"Barbecue, luv, and I told you. When the equipment truck leaves for Florida, it means spring training is right around the corner."

Winter in Woodbridge, Massachusetts can be pretty dull. With the holiday cheer packed away, the cold and early darkness felt endless, as if spring would never arrive.

Personally, I was enjoying the monotony. Almost five months earlier, I'd found myself in the middle of a murder investigation. When you're in witness protection, the last thing you want is to be in the middle of anything. Especially an investigation that threatened to undo your carefully maintained identity.

My best friend, Rob, on the other hand, was feeling antsy. Hence, he was throwing a barbecue to celebrate "Truck Day" despite it being the first week of February.

"What better harbinger of spring than pitchers and catchers reporting for duty?" he said, as he handed me a wine glass from across the kitchen island.

In honor of the occasion, he wore faded jeans and a red T-shirt emblazoned with a giant B for Boston. A backward baseball hat covered his ebony hair. As usual, he was the most handsome man in the room. When the genetic gods were dishing out beauty, Rob got two helpings.

"I can think of a few things," I told him. "The temperature going above thirty. The snow melting. You are aware that there are eight inches of snow on the ground."

"Stop being so literal. The truck is symbolic. It's like our version of a groundhog, only more reliable."

"The groundhog in Pennsylvania predicted six more weeks of winter." Jenn Falcone slid onto the stool next to mine and helped herself to the chardonnay.

"Because he's a killjoy," Rob replied. "Unlike the truck, which is always optimistic. As Robert Browning said, 'The year's at the spring. And day's at the morn.'"

"I don't understand," Jenn said. "What does Robert Browning have to do with the truck?"

"Don't worry about it. He's just showing off again."

I took the wine from her. Rob had been peppering his conversations with literary references since October. The murder investigation I mentioned earlier? The victim, Marylou Paretsky, had been gathering incriminating evidence on her friends, intending to blackmail them. As a result, the investigation tore the lid off a lot of people's secrets, including Rob's past as a boy band singer. Completely killed his mysterious millionaire professor image he had going on—face it, there's not a lot of mystique attached to dancing on stage in gold lamé. While I never would have pegged him as the insecure type, my friend seemed determined to remind everyone he was more than a pretty rich boy.

"Look, I thought a party would be a nice way to overcome the winter doldrums," Rob replied. "Everyone in the neighborhood goes into hibernation mode. No one gets together until warm weather."

"Poplar Street does," Jenn muttered from behind her glass. "They just don't include us."

I looked at Jenn, then at Rob, who shrugged.

"Whatever the reason, people seem in the mood for a party. Looks like you convinced everyone on the block to come out of their caves," I said. At least a dozen neighborhood families were represented, along with a few outsiders, like me. From outside came the screeching and laughter of the neighbor's children playing in the snow. Of course, like any party, the majority of us were gathered in the kitchen.

"Burgers and potato salad will bring out the crowds every time," he said. "By the way, you didn't borrow my jersey, did you? The replica one with the thirty-four on the back? I can't find it."

"Why on earth would I borrow your jersey?" I replied. "I don't like baseball."

"You could have borrowed it so you could be close to me when we're apart."

"Damn, you caught me. I sleep in it every night." My sarcasm earned me a sneer. I never understood why grown men wore replica jerseys in the first place. Were they expecting their favorite player to spot them in the stands and give a thumbs-up?

"It's probably hanging in Tim's closet." My son was the sports lover in the family. "Wouldn't put it past him to 'forget' he borrowed it and keep the shirt for himself."

"That would be stealing."

My breath caught. Only one man in Woodbridge had a voice that sounded like whiskey on the rocks.

Dan Bartlett—Detective Dan Bartlett—slipped his broad shoulders into the space between my stool and Jenn's. I hadn't seen him since the holidays, and my insides danced a little as his wool sweater brushed my arm. He looked good in charcoal gray. Brought out the blue in his eyes, as well as the firmness of the frame underneath. While Rob won in terms of pure physical beauty, Dan Bartlett owned the virility title. Everyone else retreated to the background whenever he entered the room.

"Surely, a fine upstanding officer like Tim wouldn't break the law," he said with a smile.

"I wouldn't be so sure. Those jerseys are expensive, and our Timmy's got a cheap streak." Rob stuck out his hand. "Glad you could make it."

"Appreciate the invite." He nodded to Jenn and then to me. "Good to see both of you again."

"Likewise," Jenn replied, flipping her ponytail. "How have you been, detective?"

"Not bad." He shot me a sly smile that, had I been standing, would have knocked me to my knees. "Your son sends his regards."

Bartlett and Tim, he of the potentially stolen jersey, worked together at the Woodbridge Police Department. By "together," I mean Bartlett outranked my patrolman son by several levels. "He also told me to remind you about drinking and driving."

Of course, he did. "Sometimes, I think Tim's trying to pay me back for all the 'smart choices' lectures I gave him when he was a child."

"I would too, considering what happened six months ago," Bartlett said.

"Six months ago was an anomaly. It's hardly a regular occurrence." Jeez, drink one cup of drugged tea and people never let you forget.

"Good to know. We'd hate to think you were a magnet for trouble."

And I hated how his gravelly voice had the habit of

sliding down my spinal column whenever he spoke. Okay, I didn't really hate it. More like I hated the way I liked the sensation.

I reached for the wine bottle, but Rob, that rat bastard, moved it out of my reach. "Dan's decided to join our spring fantasy league. I invited him over so he could meet the others," he said.

"You do fantasy sports?" That was a surprise. Bartlett struck me more as the rugged, physical type. A guy who would rather play the sport than spend his time reading stats and making virtual trades.

"Figured I'd give it a try," he said with a shrug.

"You won't be sorry," Rob told him. "We're a great bunch. Can I get you something to drink? We've got most everything."

"Except for the beer I was promised." An athletic-looking woman with too-pert-to-be-real breasts bore down on us. Diane Fitzgerald. Her suede-encased hips rolled as she strode down the hallway into the kitchen. As was often the case, her husband Alex trailed behind her, diaper bag slung over his shoulder.

I didn't know the Fitzgeralds well—they'd recently moved to Rob's neighborhood—but the few times we did meet, Diane reminded me of a blond jaguar on the hunt. But then, she was a corporate headhunter, so maybe that was required behavior. All I knew was she scared me.

Alex, though… I couldn't get a good read on him. It was almost like he was two different people. On the one hand, he came across as a try-hard. He was handsome as hell, with spiky blond hair and navy-blue eyes, but his sweaters were too tight, and he always had sunglasses perched on his head no matter what time of day it was. Just because you were middle-aged and had a washboard stomach didn't mean you had to advertise it. Look at

Bartlett. His physique was ten times better than any of them—including Rob's—and you didn't see him trying to show off.

And he flirted *a lot*. Not flirting like Rob or Jenn—flirting was like breathing to them. Alex's flirtations were kind of fake and over the top. Again, like he was trying too hard. But then, just when you were ready to write him off as a complete jerk, he'd show the other hand, and you'd catch him doing something like playing tea party with his kids.

Like I said, I couldn't figure him out.

"Honestly, Rob." Diane took her hands from her hips and hugged my friend. I think she meant the gesture to be playful, but she was too intimidating to pull it off. "I could have brewed an entire batch of beer in the bathtub by now."

"Knock it off, Diane. Not everyone's your employee. You want a drink that badly, go get one."

In my periphery, I saw Jenn's eyes widen, her expression mirroring mine. No one had ever heard Alex snap at Diane in public before.

"That's not the point," Diane replied. "Rob is the host. He's supposed to take care of my needs. I'm not going to go outside and rummage through the cooler until I find one of the good brands."

"Because you're such a brewmaster."

"I can't help it if I'm particular about what I drink."

"Puh-leeze. You don't know the difference. You're a snob."

Someone coughed. I think it was Dan Bartlett.

"I'll get you a beer, Diane," I volunteered. The deck might be warmer than the current atmosphere.

"No, I'll do it," Alex replied. "I wouldn't want you to

risk you getting the wrong kind, since Diane is so *particular*."

"While you're out there, check on the kids and make sure Greta's keeping an eye on them," Diane told him. "The other day I caught Carter trying to eat deer poop when they were in the park. I'm paying her to watch our children, not stare off into space like some absent-minded teenager."

"Don't be so hard on her, Di. She *is* a teenager."

"Of course, you'd say that, Rob. She thinks you walk on water. Check on her, Alex."

"Absolutely, Your Highness." Issuing a mock salute, he turned toward the door. As he came around the island, his hand caught Rob by the elbow. "Can I talk with you about something?"

Rob pulled his arm free. "Wings are about to come out of the oven. Everyone, prepare yourself for culinary ecstasy. Sadie, be a luv and show Dan where the drinks are."

Again, Jenn and I shared mirrored looks. That was a first. Rob Carmichael giving someone the cold shoulder. The Fitzgeralds had definitely brought a chill to the party.

Next to me, Bartlett cleared his throat. "I can find—"

"That's all right. I'll show you." Even if standing close to the man made me feel all kinds of awkward, I didn't want to appear rude. Plus, it would save me from having to make small talk with Diane. "What's your poison? Beer, wine, tequila…"

"Diet cola will work."

"That's on the deck with the beer." I hopped off the stool and motioned for him to follow me across the kitchen. The deck was a super-sized, multi-layer platform that ran along the rear of the house. When he first moved in, Rob had removed the wall between his dining room and kitchen. What he'd ended up with was a U-shaped marble counter arrangement that fed into a dining area. I like to tease Rob that the U allowed him to hold court. He could move about the middle while the rest of us either sat at the breakfast bar or the big farm-style table in the dining room. In the summer, there were two sets of sliding doors that Rob kept open, allowing guests to move freely between the spaces. Being February, he had the slider closest to the kitchen closed off, meaning traffic had to exit and enter through the dining room.

"Quite a crowd," Bartlett said as we smiled our way past a pair of mothers, both of whom felt the need to look Bartlett over. "When Rob invited me to a neighborhood barbecue, I was expecting a handful of couples. Not everyone in a half-mile radius."

"You're kidding, right? We're talking about Rob. We're lucky he didn't invite the whole town."

"You mean he didn't? Is that Darius Cook?"

I followed his gaze to the far corner of the dining room where a muscular man was holding court, his beefy hands gesturing animatedly. His size made the decorative whiskey barrel next to him look like a stepstool. "Yep. He and his wife, Toshelle, live on the next street over." I pointed to the elegant woman beside him whose long braids were tied into a ponytail that ran down the back of her gold turtleneck sweater. "Make sure you try her banana cake. It's amazing."

"I remember when he ran that interception for a touchdown in the playoffs. Phenomenal play. The guys at the station said he lived in Woodbridge."

"Works for the same law firm as Alex Fitzgerald. The guy whose wife…" I paused to think of a diplomatic word.

"The craft beer lady."

"Exactly. Anyway, I can introduce you to him—Darius —if you want."

The two of us watched as Diane, the craft beer lady herself, sidled over to the group. With a brief wave to Toshelle, she wedged herself between the Cooks and gave the strings on Darius's hoodie a tug. He, in turn, pulled her ponytail before briefly resting his hand on the base of her neck. Toshelle, I noticed, sipped her wine without changing expression.

"Maybe later," Bartlett said. "I was hoping you and I might talk."

"Really?" Goosebumps tickled my arm—from the cold air, not because his arm brushed mine when reaching around to open the slider. "What about?"

"If I didn't know better, I'd say you were trying to avoid me."

"What are you talking about? I'm not avoiding anyone. I'm getting you a drink, aren't I?"

"You know what I mean," he replied, leaning into my ear and sending my goosebumps into overdrive. "My phone calls?"

Oh, right. Those.

Okay, I *was* avoiding him. But not for the reasons he thought.

Again, it went back to the murder that occurred six months ago. Rob wasn't the only person whose past Marylou uncovered. She discovered mine as well, including my former name. I know because I found a handwritten copy of her blackmail targets, and I burned it. Destroying evidence is kind of a big no-no in police circles. I knew that because my late husband was a cop.

We stepped onto Rob's deck, where the aroma of charbroiled beef greeted our nostrils. The delicious smell undercut the feeling of snow in the air. You know, that cold, raw sensation that hung in the air when a front was due. Rob had shoveled the deck clear and lined the railing with coolers, each conveniently marked as to the contents. Soft Drinks. Traditional Beer. Craft Beer. A setup so organized that even Diane Fitzgerald wouldn't have wanted to rearrange it.

On the other side of the railing, the neighborhood kids ran around pelting each other with snowballs while Greta, she of the aforementioned deer poop failure, helped the younger children make a snowman.

"Looks like Rob," I called out. One of his baseball caps and his red cashmere scarf had been donated to the cause.

"Do you think he'll mind?" Greta called.

"That you made a snowman in his honor? Not at all. He needs hands, though. Check in the boot room by the garage. Rob might have an extra pair of gloves by the coatrack."

Hearing a soft pop, I turned to see Bartlett taking a long drink from a can of diet cola. The way his Adam's apple moved up and down... The man even made swallowing look masculine.

"It's complicated," I blurted out.

Bartlett wiped his mouth—the only reaction I got. I knew the game. He was waiting me out, staying silent until I felt the need to speak again. Which, of course, I did.

"Why I didn't return your call." Calls, actually. With an s. There had been three. "I wanted to. Call you." Had my hand on the phone the first two times. "But..."

I paused. He waited.

"It's Tim," I said. Yep, I was about to throw my son under the bus. Seriously though, what was I supposed to say? The truth? *Hey, Dan, sorry I didn't call you back, but I'm feeling guilty over this evidence I destroyed.* Like that wouldn't open a can of worms. Because, of course, Bartlett would want to know why I felt the need to destroy anything.

"You're his boss," I said.

"Not really. My department—"

"Close enough. You're his superior. It's already hard enough for him to get out from under his father's shadow. I don't want to make the situation worse."

He perched on the railing, long legs stretched in front of him, and took another swallow of soda. How his behind wasn't freezing from the contact, I didn't know. "It was dinner and a movie, Sadie, not a marriage proposal."

"Yeah, but we know what cops can be like. A police station lives on rumors," I said. "Especially in a small town. A simple dinner becomes—"

"Dammit, Stu, I said I want my money!"

The voice belonged to Alex Fitzgerald. He stood next to the grill, his fists clenched by his side. There was no mistaking the anger on his face.

Stu was Stuart Rothstein, Alex's next-door neighbor. Like Alex, Stu had a bit of a try-hard thing going on as well. In his case, I chalked it up to being a short, balding, middle-aged man whose best friends were a former pro defensive end and a Ken doll. He stood with his hands in the air.

"Dude, I warned you when you got in," he said. "This is a long-term investment. Once you're in, you're in."

"Don't *dude* me. You and I both know there are loopholes in everything. Find me one."

From out of the corner of my eye, I saw Bartlett stand up, monitoring the tension like a good peacekeeper would.

"Stu's some kind of financial guru," I said.

"Sounds like Alex isn't too happy with one of his investments," he replied.

Certainly not as far as Alex was concerned. The two

men had lowered their voices, but it was clear from Alex's face that the quarrel was far from over.

"Proving you should never do business with friends," I said. "Funny, though. The way Rob talked, I thought Stu managed a lot of Alex's investments. Guess I was wrong."

The conversation grew tenser, with the two men stepping into each other's space the way people do when feeling confrontational. Or rather, Alex stepped into Stu's space. The shorter man stopped him with a hand on his shoulder.

"Well, figure it out." Alex's voice rose again. "I need that money this week." Pushing Stu's arm away, he turned and stomped inside. Stu shrugged to the remaining two men. "…bug up his butt all week," I heard him say.

Bartlett and I parted company after that. More to the point, I begged being cold and escaped inside to avoid continuing our conversation. I had the sneaking suspicion Bartlett didn't buy my excuse, and if he decided to push, I was afraid I might trip up. I left him to chat up Darius Cook while I returned to the safety of the kitchen island and my glass of chardonnay.

On the way, I brushed past Rob, who had decided to talk with Alex after all. Telling Alex to cool off, hopefully. The two of them stood by the sink, their heads together.

Jenn waved the wine bottle as I approached. "Saw you got dumped in favor of Darius. Happens to everyone. Nick used to practically sprout wood when he saw him. What is it about guys and pro athletes that turns them into twelve-year-old boys?"

"No clue." I was too busy trying to kill the image of Jenn's ex sprouting things. "And I wasn't dumped. I showed Bartlett where the drinks were, and then I came inside."

"Uh-huh."

"Seriously."

"Whatever you say." She popped the last of a cheese puff in her mouth. I began to argue again, but a voice in my head suggested doing so might be protesting too much.

"I see Diane has inserted herself in the middle of the action as well," Jenn noted dryly. "Big surprise there."

"Excuse me?"

"She always has to have the spotlight on her. Hates it if anyone else gets the least bit of attention. I mean look at how she's practically hanging on Darius's arm and Toshelle's standing right there."

If Jenn wasn't careful, she might trip over the irony. No one flirted or enjoyed being the center of attention as much as Jenn. Other than Rob, that is.

Wow. The neighborhood was more high-maintenance than I'd realized.

"Toshelle doesn't look that upset," I said, glancing over. But then, I was more distracted by the rapture on Bartlett's face. Jenn was right; pro athletes did turn men into boys. "I'm sure she'd say something if she was."

"I think it's an alpha dog thing," Jenn continued, ignoring me. "Her way of marking the territory, so the rest of us know she's the bitch in charge."

"Who's a bitch?" Tonya Rothstein spun around, her collection of bangles clinking together as she waved her glass. Overweight by thirty or forty pounds, she had wild frizzy hair and a don't-care attitude that was the complete opposite of her husband, Stu. "If we're trashing someone in the 'hood, I want in."

"We're not trashing anyone," I said. I liked Tonya, but she was good friends with Toshelle and Diane.

"Sadie's being cranky because Dan Bartlett dumped her in favor of Darius," Jenn said.

"I'm not cranky."

"Rite of passage, Sadie. Sooner or later, every woman in the neighborhood loses their boyfriend to Darius."

"I told her the same thing," Jenn said.

Tonya wasn't listening, though. Her attention was on the group across the room. A frown creased her features. "Really wish Diane would tone it down a bit. People are going to talk."

"See?" Jenn said. "I'm not the only one who noticed how big a flirt she can be."

"Darius isn't subtle, either," I pointed out. If we were going to be criticizing, we ought to assign equal blame.

"No," Tonya agreed as she reached for the wine bottle, "he isn't."

At that moment, a loud clatter of pans made us jump. The room fell silent as everyone turned to the sink. That's where Rob and Alex Fitzgerald stood, a collection of used baking trays and cutlery scattered around their feet.

Alex immediately bent and began collecting the scattered utensils.

"Leave it," Rob snapped. I don't think I'd ever heard him speak so sharply. He'd clenched his jaw, turning his ordinarily pronounced cheekbones razor sharp. You could practically see the muscles ticking from across the room.

He bent over and yanked the utensils from Alex's hand. "Why don't you go see if your wife needs anything?"

"I'm sorry," Alex said. "I didn't mean…"

"Your wife, Alex."

The other man rose slowly. "Sorry," he said softly.

Rob glared daggers at his retreating form.

Slowly, conversation began again. Stunned, I looked at my two companions. "Wonder what that was all about," Jenn said. "Rob looks pissed."

"Tell me about it," Tonya replied. "If looks could kill, Alex would be dead."

2

THEY SAY that some people are in your lives to help you learn a lesson. If that's so, then Keith Koenig had been sent to teach me patience. Since becoming my real estate client, Keith, his wife, Debbie, and I had looked at no less than seventy-five properties. None meeting their approval.

Sunday morning found the three of us touring the best property on the market. A gorgeous four-bedroom colonial just down from Rob's house, priced to sell.

Naturally, Keith and Debbie were finding problems.

"Keith, do those windows look crooked to you?"

At Debbie's question, Keith whipped out a pocket-size level. Because of course, he carried a pocket level with him. I pressed my paper coffee cup to my forehead. It was way too early for this.

"Headache, Sadie?" Keith asked.

"Late night." While most of the families left Rob's house by nine, a few of us hung around drinking coffee and playing cards for another couple of hours. The coffee was a mistake. When I got home, I was so wired I ended up watching a cheesy cable movie instead of going to sleep.

Four and a half hours of sleep was not enough to handle the Koenigs. "Friend of mine threw a barbecue last night."

Debbie made a face. "A barbecue? In February?"

"To celebrate spring training."

"An odd reason for a party."

"It was more of an excuse for a neighborhood get-together."

"Ugh," she said, "I hate those. Why is it people think because you live on the same street, you need to be friendly? This street isn't like that, is it?"

"No. Definitely not." Lying on a Sunday. My Catholic mother would have my head. Then again, my Catholic mother was married to my mobster father, so she wasn't one to judge.

Throughout our conversation, Keith studied the windows, placing the level on one sill, then the other, and back. Suddenly he stopped. Gripping the marble counter, he leaned forward, his eyes narrowed in concentration.

"Sadie, there's something wrong," he said.

I held in a groan. "The windows aren't crooked, Keith. I promise."

"Not the windows. In the backyard. There's someone out there. I think they are hurt."

"What?" I joined him at the window. It had snowed overnight. The backyard was a pristine blanket of white.

"In the very back, behind the shed," Keith said. He pointed toward a clump of untended brush that peeked out from behind the wall. Sure enough, I saw what looked like a foot connected to a denim-clad leg.

"Call 9-1-1," I said.

While Keith dialed his cell phone, I ran out the door and across the backyard. Snow covered the leg, which was why we hadn't noticed it right away. Meaning whoever it was had been there awhile. People didn't lie around in the snow overnight unless they were seriously injured or…

I reached the edge of the shed and stopped short.

Alex Fitzgerald lay on his back with a large, dark stain across his chest, his sightless eyes facing the sky.

Damn. Not again.

"Did Rob tell you what they were arguing about?"

I shook my head. Dan Bartlett and I stood at the same window Keith Koenig had measured earlier. Outside, the well-maintained and child-friendly backyard had become a crime scene crawling with police officers and technicians. Dead bodies—particularly ones with holes in their chest—brought out the force. "I asked, but you know Rob. Said it was no big deal and waved it off."

"Yeah, he said the same thing when I asked him. You sure those were Tonya's words?"

"Yes, but it's an expression. Knocking over two pans would hardly warrant this strong a reaction. Besides, if you remember, Alex was pushing a lot of buttons last night." If we were going to be literal, Tonya's comment could apply to several people.

On the other side of the window, the police officers and technicians combed the bushes next to the woodpile. A stretcher with an empty black body bag stood nearby, a grim reminder that there was a body lying in the snow not too far away. Alex's sightless eyes stared at the sky as he waited to disappear behind the rubberized fabric.

A sour taste suddenly filled my mouth. I turned on the faucet and leaned into the stream.

Bartlett's hand rested on the space between my shoulder blades, the contact a gentle and soothing pressure. "Wouldn't a glass be easier?" he asked.

"There aren't any; the house is vacant. I'm fine now. It was the shock catching up with me. I'm not used to finding dead bodies in people's backyards."

"You're handling it like a pro. I've seen rookies lose their lunch on the spot."

His compliment was ridiculously pleasing. I'm surprised my cheeks didn't redden. I wiped my mouth on my sleeve, trying to look unaffected. Super glamorous. "What can I say? I'm tougher than I look."

"Yeah, you are." He cocked his head, his eyes oddly blue. He was doing that thing he did, where he looked into a person instead of at them. Female criminals must completely melt under the scrutiny. My insides were definitely in flux.

"What?" I asked.

He coughed, and the moment shifted. Back to business, as it were. "How well do you know the Fitzgeralds?"

"Not super well," I replied. "We've crossed paths at town functions and at Rob's house. Alex used to stop by Rob's to borrow things out of Rob's garage or drop off fantasy team stuff. Seemed like a decent guy. Hard to picture anyone wanting to kill him."

"People aren't always what they seem, Sadie. Last fall should have taught you that."

Life taught me that long before last fall, I wanted to say.

The kitchen door opened, bringing in cold air along

with my son, Tim, his lanky frame hidden under a bulky navy jacket and peaked hat. "Sorry to interrupt," he said, "but Campari found something."

At the word *something*, Bartlett stood at attention. "I'll be right there," he said. Flipping his notebook closed, he tucked it into the breast pocket of his leather jacket.

Tim stayed behind.

"What is it?" I asked, hair rising on my neck. Tim was the definition of "eager rookie". Normally he'd be following on Bartlett's heels. That he wasn't had my Mom-dar on full alert.

"It's um…what Campari found. The footprints. The victim." He rubbed his neck, and for an instant, he reminded me of his teenage self whenever he got in trouble at school. "Mom, he was coming from Uncle Rob's house."

For the second time that morning, I ran out the back door.

I found them gathered around a clump of barren forsythia bushes two yards away. I knew they were forsythia because everyone on the street had offshoots of the same forsythia plant in their backyard. Campari, a crime lab technician with a face as red as his alcohol namesake, was pointing at an object lying in the snow. On my tiptoes, I saw they were marking a section around a forsythia bush.

"Fortunately, there wasn't so much snow that we couldn't trace his footsteps," he was saying. "From the looks of things, he was stabbed at the far end of the cul-de-sac, then tried to cut through the backyards to get home. Looks like he might have paused here to catch his breath. Then he managed to stagger a couple more yards before keeling over."

"How do you know that?" I asked. "That he was stabbed at the end of the cul-de-sac?"

Every head in the police cluster turned around. Beside me, Tim groaned softly. It was one thing to let me listen in. Quite another to have me speaking up and asking questions. Especially stupid ones. I knew damn well the basis for Campari's theory, but I needed to hear him say it out loud.

Bartlett's glare pinned me to the spot. "What are you doing here?"

A reflexive question, since he no doubt had his answer as soon as he saw Tim. "We don't need bystanders contaminating the crime scene, Officer McIntyre."

Tim turned red. "I…"

"We didn't contaminate anything," I replied. "I made sure to walk in your footsteps." Did he think I'd learned nothing from being married to a police officer for sixteen years? "Besides, I'm not a bystander. I found the body." Not to mention I knew—or had given birth to—everyone standing there.

"That doesn't make you part of the investigation, Sadie."

No, but it gave me a vested interest as far as I was concerned. "Would you prefer I turn around and traipse through the crime scene?" I jerked a thumb over my shoulder. "I'm sure that won't contaminate anything."

Bartlett's sigh could be heard in Boston. "Fine. Stay. But don't talk. Finish what you were saying, Campari."

"To answer your question, Sadie, besides the obvious footprints, there's a blood trail. Not much, but enough. He was coming from the south."

Rob's house. Bartlett shot me a look. I already knew where his thoughts were going. Rob argued publicly with Alex. Now Alex was dead after what appeared to be a visit to Rob's house.

"There's something else," Campari said.

"What?" Bartlett cut me off before I could ask the same question.

Campari looked at me before giving Bartlett a dark smile. "It's better if I let you see it. Follow me."

We continued walking, with me taking great care to continue stepping in Bartlett's large footprints until we reached Rob's backyard. At that point, the single set of footprints became a dozen, thanks to the kids' snowball fight. So much for finding evidence of a backyard attack.

"Right there." Campari pointed to the snowman that reigned supreme in the center of the yard, its baseball cap and mismatched mittens still in place. As I stepped closer, my stomach sank.

A large carving knife was sticking out of the snowman's side, pink spreading across his midsection.

This wasn't good. Not good at all.

4
_____

"Bloody hell, Sadie, do you know what time it is?" It took two turns on the doorbell and pounding on the front door before Rob answered. He winced as the sunlight hit his face. From the looks of his disheveled hair and bare feet, he'd been asleep. Rob tended to sleep like the dead. No pun intended.

Noticing Bartlett standing beside me, his mouth slid into a grin. "Wasn't expecting you, detective. Something you guys want to tell me?"

"Actually…" Bartlett let the inference go unaddressed. "May we come in?"

Rob's smile faded. It was obvious the question wasn't a question. At least not one allowing for the word no. "What's wrong?"

"It's better if we talk inside," Bartlett replied.

"Sure. Hope you don't mind, but the kitchen's a mess. I left most of the cleaning until today. All of it, really."

As he stepped aside to let us pass, I noticed a bruise on his cheekbone that hadn't been there yesterday. "Looks like you hurt yourself," I remarked. Silently I prayed he had a good explanation.

"Did I?" His fingers brushed his cheek. "Must have done it when I was coming in from my run. Slipped and smacked my face on the front railing. Got a matching one on my rear end. I'd show you, but I don't want to fluster Dan here."

He closed the door and led us down the marble hallway toward the rear of the house, stopping to adjust a painting. "Gonna be straightening up for the next week. What's up?"

Dan was busy making note of the crooked frame and the rest of the surroundings. "I'm afraid I've got some bad news," he said.

"Bad how? What the—" Rob stopped short in the kitchen hallway. "Why are there a bunch of policemen crawling around my backyard?"

"I wouldn't say crawling," I said.

"That's the bad news," Bartlett said at the same time. "Maybe you should take a seat."

He motioned to the seats Jenn and I had occupied the night before. From over Rob's shoulder, I spied a countertop filled with serving bowls and used wine glasses. Looking over the clutter for Rob's knife set, I spied the block tucked behind a half-full bowl of potato chips.

The carving knife slot was empty.

"Mind if I make some coffee? I'm still waking up."

I opened my mouth to reply, but this time Bartlett managed to speak first. "It'd be better if you sat down. Both of you," he added with a glance at me.

Since Bartlett was already breaking police protocol by letting me be there, I did what he said, grabbing Rob by the arm and yanking him onto the stool next to me. Creases marked his forehead as he looked between us.

"Okay, what's up?" he asked. "Why are there cops rooting around my rhododendrons? Did something happen? Oh, Lord." He groaned and washed a hand over his features. "Please don't tell me someone got into an accident on the way home. I swear I kept an eye on alcohol consumption."

"It wasn't an accident," I told him.

"Then…"

"How well do you know Alex Fitzgerald?" Bartlett asked.

"How well do I know him?" Rob swiveled his chair, his gaze fixed on the plate of crumbs in front of him. "We're friendly enough. We're in the same fantasy leagues. Why?"

Bartlett had taken out his trusty notepad and was writing notes. "You argued with him last night. About what?"

"An argument? Last night?"

The way Rob insisted on repeating Bartlett's questions was making me uneasy. Reminded me of someone playing for time.

Why? What did he have to hide?

Bartlett had noticed, too. His blue eyes took on that intense sheen they got whenever he was assessing a situation. "When the pans fell on the floor," he said.

"Oh, that. I wouldn't call that an argument, exactly. More of a difference in opinion."

"About what?" Bartlett repeated.

"About what?" Definitely delaying. "Alex wanted to invite this guy from his firm to join our league, and I told him I thought the guy was a major tool."

"And the pans?"

"I hit them with my elbow when I turned around." Rob's shrug was overly blasé. "It wasn't a big deal."

"Why was he grabbing your arm, then?" I asked.

"He grabbed my arm?"

"Yeah." This repeating thing was getting on my nerves. How did Bartlett stand it?

Speaking of, I shot the detective a look before continuing. "He looked like he didn't want you walking away from the conversation."

"I don't remember that."

Bull. Rob and I had been friends way too long; I knew all his tics. In this case—if the repetition routine hadn't already given him away—it was the way his middle and index fingers moved in a plucking motion. Playing an imaginary bass guitar.

My heel began to bounce in response. Jittery legs were my nervous tic.

Meanwhile, Rob was once again looking between Bartlett and me. "Why are you so interested in my row with Alex? And what does any of this have to do with my yard?" Rob asked.

"He's dead," Bartlett said.

Rob's eyes and mouth widened in disbelief. "Wha-what?"

What little color his face had left drained away, and he slumped forward into the counter. He looked like someone punched him in the gut, only instead of doubled over, he was folded around the edge of his quartz counter. "I can't believe... Are-are you sure?" he asked. "I mean, that it's Alex?"

"We're sure," Bartlett replied. "When's the last time you saw him?"

"Last night, same as you," Rob told him. "Christ, Diane, and the kids must be shattered." He wiped a hand across his mouth, swearing softly between his fingers. I stole a look over my shoulder at Bartlett, who was jotting in his notebook. Had he noticed the same thing I had? That Rob hadn't asked how Alex had died?

Of course, he had. Bartlett noticed everything. The knot in my stomach tightened. Hopefully, Rob's omission was from shock and nothing more.

"Do you know what time he left?" Bartlett asked.

Rob shook his head. "I'm not sure. He was still here when you left, I think."

"That was eight-thirty. I happened to see the clock," I added when Bartlett arched his brow.

"Alex left maybe fifteen or twenty minutes later," Rob said. "Diane asked him to go home and check on Greta and the kids."

Both Bartlett and I nodded. Greta had taken a whiny Carter and Natalie home shortly after dinner. "And Diane stayed at the party without him?" Bartlett asked.

"She was busy talking with the Cooks and the Roth-steins. It wasn't unusual," he added. "Alex was usually the one who checked on the kids."

Bartlett had moved on, more interested at the moment in Alex's comings and goings so he could build a timeline of events. "And what time did they all leave? Diane and the others."

"I'm not sure. They stuck around for a couple of rounds of cards. I…um…" Rob rubbed his forehead. "I started a card game to rescue Sadie from Jim Chu. He had her cornered."

"That the tall, good-looking guy I saw you talking to when I left?"

He'd noticed? Was that why he hadn't said goodbye? "I made the mistake of asking how his new job was going. Guy had me trapped forever while he pontificated on the merits of solar heating." An hour of my life I wouldn't get back. "Thank God for cards."

"Night baseball," Rob said. "Thought it thematic."

"What time was this?" Bartlett asked.

"Probably around nine. Diane and the others, I think, left around nine-thirty or ten. Party broke up around an hour later."

"And you didn't see Alex after that?"

"I went out for a run... God, I can't believe this." Pushing himself from the stool, Rob made his way, still barefoot, to the middle of the kitchen where he stopped and stared out the slider door. I followed him. Outside, investigators were photographing the snowman. The red streak was more prominent from this angle. I could see where it started in the middle of the stomach. One of the arms was broken off, too. The left one. Had Alex grabbed at the snowman for balance as he stumbled away?

Rob noticed the streak, too. He let out another groan. "Oh God, is that..."

"They don't know what it is," I replied. The police were presuming, but maybe the streak wasn't blood at all. There'd been kids everywhere at the party. Maybe one of them spilled fruit punch. Then wiped it like a bloody hand streak across the snowman.

Stranger things had happened, right?

"Is that why you're asking me questions? Are you saying, Alex...?"

"I need to ask again, Rob," Bartlett said. "Did you see Alex after he left the party? He didn't return after the card game?"

"I..."

The investigator closest to the window looked up and saw us watching. Taking Rob by the arm—again—I turned him around. He moved with compliancy, not at all Rob-like. The Rob I knew was a perpetual energy machine, always chatting and spreading sunshine. This version stared out the window with a distant frown, his eyes vacant.

"I don't know," he finally answered Bartlett's question. "I mean, maybe? I told you, I went for a run."

Even with my back to him, I could tell Bartlett was arching his brow as he asked. Hell, I was arching mine. Who the hell runs at eleven p.m.?

"I thought it might clear my head and help me sleep," Rob replied as though reading our thoughts.

"You do that often?"

"Run? Sure. All the time. You know that."

"In the middle of the night?"

"Sometimes, if I need to clear my head or I'm stressed."

Bartlett looked at me for confirmation, and I shrugged. It was the first I'd heard of the habit. He nodded and jotted something in his notebook, his pen making scratching sounds in the silence. "What was the reason last night?"

"A little bit of both. I needed to decompress after the party. I get pretty jacked up after a social event, especially if I've had a few."

"How far did you go?"

"Oh, jeez, I don't know." Rob ran a hand over his stubble. "Seven, maybe eight miles. I ran to the cemetery, looped around Auburndale Street, and came home. Slipped on my front step and decided to go straight to bed. Figured the cleaning could wait till morning."

More silence. More scratching of Bartlett's pen. "Anyone see you?" he asked after a moment.

"A couple of cars, maybe. Not many people around that time of night, unless you count the ones in the graveyard."

Just then, Rob's cell phone, which lay on the kitchen

bar played the fail sound from *The Price Is Right*. "That's Jenn," Rob said. "She must have seen the police and wants to know what's going on. I'll call her later. I can't deal with her right now."

"Might be a good idea to turn your phone off and not talk to anyone for a while," Bartlett said.

Rob looked between us. "Why?"

Before he could answer, there was a knock on the patio door. From the other side, Campari and another investigator waved for attention. From the urgent expressions on their faces, they'd found something.

Bartlett grimaced. "I'll be right back," he said. "Don't touch anything while I'm gone." If he was worried about Rob disturbing the scene, he needn't. Rob hadn't moved.

"Either of you," he added, turning a pointed blue stare in my direction.

Oh.

All right, that was fair. I'd worry about me trying to protect Rob by wiping away incriminating evidence if I were in his shoes, too.

I mean, it's not like I hadn't destroyed evidence before.

For the time being, however, I was more interested in getting information than I was in destroying it. My bestie was holding back about something, and I needed to know what.

As soon as Bartlett stepped outside, I grabbed Rob's arm and dragged him through the kitchen doorway and into the living room. It was a testimony to my friend's state of mind that he went so willingly. I pushed him onto the sofa, stood over him, and gave him my sternest, most probing look. The one I used to give Tim when he came home late from curfew.

"Talk," I said.

"Talk about what?"

Nice try, but I'd raised a teenager; I knew when someone was playing dumb. I doubled down on my glare. "For starters? How 'bout explaining why you lied to the police?"

5

HE LOOKED at me with tired eyes. "I don't know what you're talking about."

"The hell you don't. I saw the look on your face when you and Alex had that dust-up in the kitchen. No way were you talking about fantasy football."

"Baseball."

"Whatever," I said. "That wasn't a disagreement. You two were close to blows."

"No, we weren't," he replied in a subdued voice. He looked at his hands which hung, loosely clasped, between his knees. "I would never hit Alex. And I wasn't angry, not like you think. I was…" He breathed out loudly through his nose. "I was frustrated."

I sat next to him. "About what?" What was he keeping to himself?

"I-I'm sorry, Sadie, but it's not something I want to talk about."

It was my turn to breathe loudly. Normally, I couldn't care less if someone wanted to keep a secret. We all had things we didn't want to share with the world. Considering the information I'd kept buried the past two decades, it'd be mighty hypocritical of me to insist others bare all to the world.

But these weren't normal circumstances. "Sweetie, I don't think you're grasping the seriousness of all this. Alex was *murdered*. He was stabbed with an expensive kitchen knife, and footprints track him to your yard. And you lied to the police! Don't try to argue; it was obvious. You suck under pressure," I added when he opened his mouth to retort. "If I noticed, you don't think Bartlett noticed, too?"

"Bloody hell." Giving a groan, he buried his face in his hands. "I'm screwed, aren't I?"

"Not necessarily, although lying and holding back information doesn't help."

He lifted his head. "Says the woman who destroyed Marylou Paretsky's blackmail list."

Touché. "That was a huge mistake. And, if you remember, Bartlett figured out about Marylou's schemes anyway. He'll find out what you're hiding, too." I reached over and covered his hands with one of mine. "Talk to me. Tell me what's going on, and maybe I can help you figure out a way around it."

"I don't know, Sadie. It's not my secret to tell."

"Well, I doubt Alex is going to be saying anything." Crass, yes, but my loyalty at the moment was with the man on the sofa. Seeking to soften the remark, I added, "And, if he were still alive, I doubt he'd want to see you in trouble for his problems."

"Don't be so sure," Rob replied. "Especially if it meant Diane and his family finding out."

"Not even to help a friend?" What kind of secret would he share with Rob that he couldn't share with the police or his family?

Oh. *That* kind of secret. "Are you telling me that you and he…"

"No!"

His protest was a little *too* forceful, and, from the way he immediately looked down, he knew it.

I studied his profile. Even hungover and stubbled, he was a beautiful man. "Rob, Alex is dead and there are police in your backyard. As much as Bartlett is a friend, he's going to ferret out the truth."

"We kissed," he said finally.

"I gathered it was something like that. When?"

"About a month ago. He came over to watch football. We had a half dozen beers, got tipsy, and were messing around when all of a sudden, he leaned in and kissed me. Said it was something he'd been contemplating doing for a while."

"By kiss, I'm guessing you don't mean a quick peck."

"Hard to peck with your tongue."

Yeah, I imagined it was. "So, Alex was bisexual."

"Technically, yes, but he didn't enjoy the wasn't happy with the choices he'd made," Rob replied. "You know, wife. Kids. He made those decisions to please his father more than anything."

From what little I knew, Alex's father had been a successful college athlete who'd gone on to become a successful lawyer. Like founding-member-of-a-fancy-law-firm successful.

"His dad was caught up in the whole arrogant, masculine identity thing," Rob continued. "He expected Alex to follow suit. Being gay didn't fit with the plan."

"And yet, he kissed you."

"Said he was tired of fighting the attraction, and I…" He looked at the floor. "I was, too."

"You were?"

"I know what you're thinking, but when it was the two of us when he relaxed and dropped the super-cool act, he was really nice. Smart. Funny. Gentle."

The kind of guy who played tea party with his kids.

"Anyway, I told him I didn't do the closeted husband thing, and he gave me this spiel about how his lifestyle could accommodate his marriage and our relationship. Wanted to have his cake and eat it too, he did. I told him no. I didn't want to be his dirty little secret. I thought, given everything he had at stake, that would be the end."

"But it wasn't the end, was it?"

"No. Alex could be damn persistent when he wanted to be. Persuasive."

A small sad smile tugged at his mouth. Remembering. Didn't take a genius to guess they'd shared more than a single kiss. A lot more.

"He started coming over after Diane and the kids went to bed. We would spend hours going around and around, talking about his father and his family. He'd make promises, and then change his mind the next day. Come up with a reason why he couldn't. I finally told him he had to make up his mind once and for all. What he was doing wasn't fair to Diane."

"Or you."

"Or me." He scratched at the fabric on his knee. "You must think I'm a terrible person, getting involved with a married man."

"No." A little hurt he hadn't confided in me, but considering the secrets I hid, I wasn't in a position to judge.

Through the doorway, I could see Bartlett and Campari kneeling on the patio. Campari was snapping pictures. Not a good sign.

"The argument you two had." Suddenly Rob's pointed comments made sense.

"More of the same. He pulled me aside and told me that this time he was definitely leaving Diane. I didn't believe him and told him to leave me alone. I didn't talk to him for the rest of the night." His voice cracked on the last part.

"Did you know he was coming back?"

He shook his head. "No, but I was afraid he might. That's why I went for a run. If I'd stuck around, maybe…" His features crumpled.

Oh, Rob. I wrapped him in a hug. "You didn't know. You *couldn't* know."

"Thing is, it wasn't about him being with me. I wanted him to be honest about who he was. No one should live a lie."

Not unless they had to. I hugged him a little tighter. "You need to tell Bartlett everything."

"But Diane and the kids…."

"Right now, you've got bigger things to worry about than protecting them."

"Sorry to interrupt." Bartlett stood in the doorway. He looked as tall and imposing as ever, but there was an uncharacteristic slump in his shoulders. His gravelly voice sounded tired and heavy. "Do you want to tell me how the blood got on your patio, Rob?"

Much bigger problems.

6

"THERE'S no way he killed anybody," I said a short time later. "No way in hell."

I was preaching to the choir since it was Tim sitting on the opposite side of the table. We were sitting at a table in Cuppa Joe's Café, the town's favorite coffee shop. I'd been ranting since Bartlett brought Rob to the police station. For additional questions, he'd said.

Which meant, *Get a lawyer; you're a suspect.*

"For crying out loud, we're talking about your Uncle Rob," I said. "The man teaches British Literature."

"He also sang in a boy band," Tim said. "Neither makes him incapable of violence."

With an expression way too reminiscent of his father, he eyeballed me over his paper coffee cup. Black coffee. Big change from the man who used to add five sugars. "How many times did Dad say that anyone can be a murderer when they're pushed?"

"But this is Rob."

It was the best argument I had at the moment. Either

that or mentioning my gut, which was certain he didn't hurt anyone. Sure, Rob could be sarcastic, and obnoxious, and he flirted with anyone or anything that walked, but he had the soul of a poet. The guy could barely make it through one of those SPCA commercials without tearing up.

He'd also been there when my husband, Jack, died. Held me during those dark early days. Helped me return to the land of the living a month later. Played surrogate father when Tim needed one. He was my handsome, cheeky Rock of Gibraltar; he wasn't a killer.

"He helped pin your badge when you graduated the academy, and when you received your commission in the Guard."

"I get it, Mom. He's family." Looking at his coffee, he flicked at the lip of the plastic cover with his thumb, the motion making a soft *click-click-click* sound. "For what it's worth, I have trouble picturing him hurting anyone either. But the evidence doesn't look good. I mean…" He leaned forward and lowered his voice. "They found freaking blood at his house. And the knife."

"I know, I know." The evidence was stacked against him. At the moment. "Obviously, we're going to have to find additional evidence if we're going to prove his innocence."

I might as well have said I was going to fund Rob's getaway by hitting a bank. Tim immediately drew his features into a scowl.

I hated it when he scowled. Reminded me of his birth father—a nasty-tempered thug from whom I'd spent the past twenty-five years in hiding. Fortunately, Tim didn't know about his birth father. Most of his mannerisms—as well as his love for law enforcement—he'd gotten from his adopted father. Now and then, though, he would make a face or speak in a certain tone, and I'd remember where he came from. Scowling was one of those faces.

In this case, I knew exactly what he was scowling about, too. "Please do not start poking around this case," he said. It wasn't a request, despite the word *please*.

"And why not?" I sat back in my seat as well. "Someone has to look out for Rob."

"Yeah, and that someone is called the police. Do you remember what happened the last time you played amateur detective? You were nearly killed."

"But I wasn't," I replied, "and I learned from the incident."

"That's supposed to make me feel better?"

"You can feel whatever you want. Consider it payback for all those times you decided to worry me by staying out past your curfew to fool around with Emily Swanton."

"Mom! I did not fool around with Emily Swanton." His tomato-colored cheeks said otherwise. "Besides, it's not the same thing. This is a murder investigation. If Uncle Rob is innocent—"

"If?"

He countered my raised eyebrow with another scowl. "You know what I mean. If there's evidence, the police will find it."

Since in this case, "the police" meant Dan Bartlett, my kid had a point. Bartlett wouldn't rush to judgment; it wasn't his style. "They will find no evidence because your Uncle Rob is innocent," I told him.

"You're right. Uncle Rob will be cleared in no time." His reassurance lacked enthusiasm, though.

I suppose I couldn't blame him. I was a civilian and therefore allowed to go on blind faith. Tim, on the other hand, was a cop, trained to put his personal feelings aside and study the evidence, which at the moment, was pretty damning.

This was hard for him. I could see the conflicting emotions in the way he stared into his coffee. "Let's talk about something else," I told him. "I need a distraction." We both did. "When does that new officer start?" Woodbridge had recently hired a new academy graduate, meaning Tim was no longer the rookie. He was looking forward to someone else getting the hazing and grunt hours.

"This week," he replied. "She's supposed to be riding along with Vasquez for the month."

"Congrats on no longer being the new guy."

He managed a smile. "Gotta admit, it'll be nice to have someone beneath me for a change. Oh-oh."

"What?" I looked over my shoulder to see Dan Bartlett filling the doorway. His eyes scanned the room before settling on our table. On me. Upset as I was that he'd taken Rob into custody, my stomach still fluttered.

Damn him.

He cut through the room until he reached us. "Aren't you supposed to be at the station, Officer McIntyre?"

"My shift ended a few hours ago," Tim replied. "Mom was upset about Uncle…this morning…so I thought I'd let her talk it out. We were just finishing up."

"And are you feeling better?" Bartlett asked me. "Stumbling over a dead body can be pretty traumatic."

"I'll survive. I've got other issues to worry about."

His mouth played with the idea of frowning, then changed its mind and remained a straight line. "I imagine you do. Mind if I sit?"

"Don't you have a suspect to interrogate?" I asked as

he pulled a chair up to the table. Across the way, Tim stiffened.

"The *person of interest* is meeting with his lawyer so I'm giving him privacy."

Raising his hand, he signaled for Carlos, the barista behind the register, who, annoyingly, waved back.

"Morning, detective," he called over. "The usual?"

"And a large… Hold on. What does Rob usually order?"

"You're buying him coffee?"

"Guy looks like he could use the caffeine."

"Can you blame him?" I asked. "He's sitting in an interrogation room."

"That's where all sus- people of interest sit."

Too late, he'd already slipped. Rather than gloat—as much as I wanted to—I reached for my cup instead.

"A large latte, extra foam," Tim hollered to Carlos.

"Thank you," Bartlett said. To me, he added, "I'm not enjoying this. I happen to like Rob, but I can't ignore—"

"If you're going to lecture me about the evidence, you can save your breath. Tim already has." Frankly, the word was beginning to give me a headache.

"Good. Then you realize I had no choice."

Since I was pouting into my coffee cup when he spoke, I looked up at him through my lashes. Yet again, I was struck by the slight slump in his usually rigid shoulders. And while his was never a face that wore emotions, his eyes did look a little weary.

"Taking an extra-long break, are we, Officer McIntyre?" he asked, looking at Tim.

Immediately, my son sat up straighter. One thing about my son, he respected authority. Definitely not something he got from his bio dad. "I'm off," he said. Bartlett must really be preoccupied. Tim had already said he was off duty.

"Well, you're on again. I need you to deliver that latte to the station."

"Seriously?"

Bartlett's face was stone serious. "Do you have a problem with taking Mr. Carmichael a coffee?"

"I…" He looked between us, before changing his answer. "No, sir. I'll take care of it right now."

"Was that necessary?" I asked once Tim hustled away. "He's been up all night."

"He won't be the first cop to lose sleep for a case, you know that. Besides, I need to talk to you, and I'd rather he not be present."

"Why is that?" I asked. That he looked at me with the same stony face, made my stomach drop. "This is official, isn't it?" I had a feeling I knew the topic, too. Rob had told him about Alex.

Bartlett didn't answer right away. He waited while Tim dropped off a cup of mint tea. "Carlos said he'd add the drinks to your tab," Tim said in a flat voice. He was trying not to sound upset at being dismissed.

"Thank you," Bartlett said. "You better get that coffee to the station before it grows cold. Your Uncle Rob will be glad to see it."

The coffee or Tim? My nerves were temporarily supplanted by a warm fuzzy feeling as I realized Bartlett was providing Rob with a friendly face. He might hide it well, but Bartlett had a soft side. Whenever I caught a glimpse, the center of my chest expanded a little. Tender and tough was a dangerously attractive combination.

However, the feeling was short-lived. As soon as Tim was out the door, Bartlett suggested we leave as well. "I'll walk you to your car," he said. "We can talk on the way."

On a different occasion, I might be annoyed at being dragged from my seat before I was ready, but not this time. If we were discussing Rob and Alex, I'd rather protect Rob's privacy. Cuppas was a petri dish for town gossip. All it would take was one person to overhear, and Rob's private life would be blasted all over town. His boy-band past was already public knowledge. He didn't need more tawdry tales following him.

We stepped outside to a bright winter sun. The last of the storm clouds had receded into the distance, meaning the approaching afternoon would be at least sunny if not warmer. A faint mint aroma drifted in the air. Bartlett had peeled the tab on his cup.

"How are you feeling?" he asked, as we made our way through the parking lot of dark SUVs.

"My best friend is under arrest for murder. How do you think I feel?" While I spoke, I kicked a hunk of fallen snow that had fallen off someone's undercarriage. It burst into several smaller chunks that sprayed in different directions.

"He not under arrest. He's a person of interest."

I rolled my eyes. The two terms were interchangeable for cops. "Fine. My best friend is *a person of interest*. Doesn't change how I feel."

"I didn't think it would. For what it's worth, I don't like what's happening any more than you do. Rob is my friend, too. Do you think I enjoyed asking him downtown?"

No, I didn't imagine he did. And he was, I had to admit, treating Rob better than other suspects. At least I'd never seen him get a latte for anyone else. "That was nice of you to send Tim with the latte," I said. My version of an olive branch. "Thank you."

Bartlett shrugged. "I told you, I didn't want your son around for this conversation."

"I know." Though he could have gotten me alone if he wanted.

We walked the next three yards in silence. Finally, he turned to look at me and asked, "How long have you known about Rob and Fitzgerald?"

7

THERE WAS challenge in his eyes. Annoyance that I might
have held out on him. "I didn't know anything until today.
He told me when you were outside on his deck."

The challenge faded, but only slightly. "What exactly
did he tell you?"

"That it was more of a strong, mutual attraction than
an actual fling. Rob told Alex he had to stop coming over
because he didn't do married men, but Alex was persistent,
and that was the reason behind last night's argument."

"In other words, it was all Alex, and Rob was the
virtuous man being courted."

"Is that so hard to believe?" I asked. "Half the town
has a crush on Rob, maybe more. Plus, he has scruples. No
way would he get involved with a married man."

"When's the last time he was involved with anyone?"
Bartlett asked.

"About two years ago. Some guy with the BSO. They
dated for six months." Since then, he'd been lying low.

"It's been a dry spell then," Bartlett remarked.

"What, we're going to start assessing people's guilt

based on their sex lives? If so, you might as well bring me in for questioning, too."

Somehow the comment didn't sound as sarcastic and cutting out loud as it did in my head. "You know what I mean," I said when Bartlett started to smirk. "A dry spell doesn't mean Rob's ripe for an extramarital affair."

"Maybe not, but unfortunately, the only person who can confirm his version of the story is dead. You've got to admit, without evidence to the contrary, this could easily be seen as a spurned lover lashing out."

"Evidence, schmevidence," I muttered. He knew as well as I did that circumstantial evidence didn't always tell the whole story.

"Hey! Did I say I was done investigating?" His gloved hand slipped into mine and gave my fingers a squeeze. He had a firm, steady grip. "If I've learned anything over the years, it's that things aren't always as obvious as they seem. Trust the process, okay?"

"Okay," I said.

Bartlett was right. This was only the start of the investigation. There was evidence out there that implicated the real killer. It was only a matter of time before it was discovered.

"Atta girl," he said.

Wow. I hadn't heard that phrase in years. My late husband used to say the same phrase when we first met, when I was a pregnant, scared witness and he was a New York cop assigned to keep an eye on me. *Atta girl*, he would say, whenever I tackled something scary, and my stomach would give a little bounce knowing I'd earned his approval.

Hearing Bartlett say it, my stomach bounced again.

He gave my fingers a final squeeze and released my hand. Immediately, I flexed my fingers, eager to keep the steadying warmth from fading. "In the meantime," he said, "don't do anything foolish, okay?"

Et tu, Bartlett? "Don't worry, I won't," I replied.

Of course, the word *foolish* meant different things to different people. Wasn't my fault if we had different definitions, was it?

8

"DIANE."

It was later in the day, and I was on the phone with Tim. Even though it was Sunday, I was sitting at my desk at Renee Drake Realty. Prospective homebuyers who work during the week don't care if you spent the morning dealing with a murder; they want to tour houses. And so, despite everything, I spent my day with clients. In between appointments, however, I ran through various scenarios.

"Surely, she has as much motive for killing Alex as anyone," I told my son. I had it all worked out in my head. Diane could have followed Alex to Rob's house. They argued, and, in a fit of passion, she stabbed him using the first weapon she could find.

"That's pure speculation," Tim said after I laid out my theory.

"No more than thinking Rob did it. And Diane's far more ruthless." I could see her thrusting a carving knife into someone's chest.

"Why would she have followed him to Uncle Rob's in the first place?"

"Because." I stopped, thinking of Rob's confession. I didn't want to break his confidence. On the other hand, Tim would learn the truth soon enough. Rob knew better than to lie during an official interrogation.

"Because she suspected something was up between Alex and your Uncle Rob," I said.

On the other end of the line, the sounds of the station mingled with Tim's breath. He was rocking in his seat; I could hear the springs squeaking. "Was there?"

"Not the way you're thinking. Rob doesn't do married men. But there was an attraction. If Diane suspected? Or thought her marriage was in jeopardy? Well, there's a motive."

Tim's breath sounded in my ear.

"What?"

"It's also a possible motive for Uncle Rob," he said. "Alex comes over to end things. The two argue, and Rob stabs him with the first weapon he could find."

"But he didn't." The plausibility of his theory made me shiver. I didn't want to think about it. "Seems to me we could at least ask Diane where she was last night."

"We?" Tim repeated. "I thought you were going to behave yourself."

"Slip of the tongue. I meant you. Although now that you mention it, losing your husband's attention to another man could be embarrassing. She might share more in a less official atmosphere."

"Mom…"

"Relax. I didn't say I was going to drive over to her house and confront the woman," I said. Give me some credit for subtlety. "I meant that when it comes to marital issues, people might be more comfortable chatting with a friend. Or at least an acquaintance."

"We don't need her to have a friend right now. We need you to let us do our job."

I grit my teeth. Someone forgot who he was talking to. "Don't go using that *us* and *we* stuff with me, mister. I'm not some regular outsider. I was helping your dad with his cases when you were still playing with your stuffed animals."

"Dinner table conversation is not the same thing."

"As what?" Helping? It damn well was the same thing. Jack McIntyre had relied on my insight all the time, and Tim knew it.

Luckily, Tim was smart enough to recognize when he was about to dig himself a hole. "Never mind. Just don't do something foolish, okay?"

Him too? "Of course," I replied. Again, the concept of *foolish* was open to interpretation.

There was a pause while he had a muffled conversation with someone. "I've got to go. I'll call you later and give you an update. Okay?"

"Thank you," I said. "Love you."

"Me too. Bye." The line when dead.

"So, who does Number One Son not want you to confront?"

I jumped. Speaking of scary, alpha females... Renee Drake plopped herself into the chair next to my desk.

Renee might be the one person I knew who was shrewder and more intimidating than Diane. Woodbridge's top real estate agent—the top agent in the area actually—had built her empire with a level of street smarts and hustle that would make even the top success moguls jealous.

She was also the reason I had a real estate career in the first place, mediocre though it may be. After Jack died, she told me I could have a job if I got my Realtor's license. To this day I'm not sure if it was out of sympathy or because she felt she owed me for all the years her son, Hilty, practically lived at our house. He and Tim had been joined at the hip since they were six years old.

Now that I thought about it, Renee did owe me.

At the moment, she was fixing me with hawk-sharp eyes. Her gray and tangerine pantsuit was a lesson in power dressing as was her short, spiky hair. "If you and another agent are having a turf war," she started. "Check that. You being in a turf war would mean you're finally being aggressive. Who are you fighting with, and why does Tim care?"

"I'm not fighting with anyone," I said, ignoring how my answer made her plumped lips frown with disappointment. "Although if someone wants to poach Keith, I won't complain."

"Don't tell me the Koenigs passed on Evergreen Lane? That kitchen is to die for."

Bad choice of words. "I take it you haven't heard."

"Heard what?" she asked, her frown growing more pronounced. "I've been buried in paperwork and showings all day."

I told her about finding Alex's body. Normally, Renee wasn't one for dramatic responses, but when I finished, her jaw dropped.

"No way," she said. "He was lying in the snow?"

"Yep." I could still picture the scene. Probably would for a long time.

"Wow." She ran her fingers through her short, dark hair. "Do they know who did it?"

"Not yet. They're talking to a person of interest, but it's too early for them to have anyone concrete in mind." Bending the truth slightly, perhaps, but until news about

Rob became public, I was going to do what I could to shield him.

Renee shook her head. "Unbelievable. I can't believe Alex Fitzgerald is dead. I sold them their home."

No surprise there. Directly or indirectly, Renee had a hand in almost every home sale in Woodbridge. "Right after their daughter was born. Or was it their son? Babies tend to look alike to me."

"Probably their son, Carter," I said. "Natalie is older."

"Whatever. What I do remember is that they handled everything without a lawyer."

Picturing Diane and Renee going toe-to-toe during inspections, I shuddered. "That must have been fun."

"Actually, it was one of the easiest sales I've ever had. They were eager to move into that neighborhood. Made an offer on the house before it came on the market. Ten-k over asking price.

"No kidding." I'd pictured them negotiating every little point in their favor. "Guess they were eager. Did they say why?"

"I think they were super good friends with Stu and Tonya Rothstein. I sold them their house, too. Tonya was the one who tipped Diane off about the house going on the market."

"Really?" I knew they were good friends, but I'd had no idea the relationship predated the Fitzgeralds moving in.

"Yeah. Now that I think about it, I've sold nearly every house on that street. Such a great neighborhood. I wonder if Diane will stay there now that it's only her and the kids."

"Renee! The woman hasn't been a widow for twenty-four hours. I doubt relocation is on her mind." Establishing an alibi, maybe, but not relocating.

"I didn't think she was putting the house on the market this week. I meant in the future. That street is a hot one."

"The dead body one street over might kill some of the desirability factor," I replied.

"Only if you let it, Sadie. A crime scene can be a great selling point if you spin it right."

"Selling point to whom? Ted Bundy?" Only Renee would think murder made for a good marketing angle. *The house comes with central air, granite counters, and its very own chalk outline.*

"Hold that thought," I said as my phone rang. "Renee Drake Realty. Let us take you home." The corny tagline Renee insisted we use stumbled off my tongue. I often "forgot" to say it, but with Renee standing over me, I couldn't. "Sadie McIntyre speaking."

"Renee Drake, please."

Every caller asked for Renee. They all wanted to work with Number One. What most people didn't realize was that Renee stayed Number One by taking on only those customers who had big houses or big budgets. The rest of us survived on her crumbs.

"May I tell her who's calling?"

"My name is Theresa Crowe."

I scribbled her name on the intake form and showed it to Renee who shook her head. My insides sagged. Normally, I looked forward to crumbs, but today I was more interested in learning more about Diane Fitzgerald. "Renee's showing a property at the moment." One of our go-to screening lines. "May I help you?"

"My partner Christopher and I would like to buy a house. Preferably as soon as possible." Her voice had a stilted, studied sound, almost British, but not quite. The kind of voice you'd associate with a difficult client.

"Do you have a specific property you're interested in?"

"Isn't it your job to recommend properties to us?"

"Absolutely." Thank goodness she couldn't hear teeth clenching over the phone. "Let me get some information so I can pull up the listings that fit your needs. Let's start with the basics. Where are you living now?"

"Winter Street," she replied.

The street name sounded familiar, but I couldn't place it. Unlike Renee, I couldn't recall every street and house in Woodbridge. I could, however, tell the difference between a baby boy and a baby girl.

"We can't wait to leave this neighborhood so don't show us anything near this address," the woman continued. "Christopher and I want a home where there's privacy."

"No problem. There are some wonderfully private neighborhoods in Woodbridge."

"Good. I can be at your office in half an hour to review them. Will you be there?"

For a moment, I thought about lying and telling her no, but again, Renee was standing over me listening. "Sounds good. See you then." After additional questions, I hung up the phone with a sigh.

"Don't get too excited," Renee remarked. "You might hurt yourself."

"Sorry. She sounds like she's going to be another Keith Koenig and give me headaches."

"They can't all be gems."

Maybe so, but they didn't all have to be problem children, either. "I was hoping to get out of here a little early, that's all. I had something I wanted to do."

Renee tossed her tangerine scarf over her shoulder. "Real estate doesn't take Sundays off, you know that."

Neither did murder. Unfortunately, only one paid my mortgage, meaning I was stuck with Theresa.

9

"ARE you sure those are the only properties available?" Theresa asked me as we settled at my desk.

My new client didn't match her voice. She was a waif of a woman with sharp features and a mane of curls that she wore pulled back by a headband. Her navy blue pea coat had dog hair all over it and a rainbow pin on the lapel. A white Bichon Poodle sat on her lap.

"Just about," I replied. I'd shown her four houses, including one slightly above her price range and she'd been underwhelmed by the selection. So much for wanting to buy ASAP. Her partner Christopher was apparently quite selective. He was also quite charming, quite handsome, quite smart, and quite perfect or so I'd gleaned from her running monologue.

"I'm afraid we're a little low on inventory at the moment," I told her.

"What a shame. Christopher and I were hoping to find something quickly."

The dog, who was not Christopher, I'd discovered, barked in agreement.

From inside her office, Renee loudly cleared her throat. I knew why. There was one listing I hadn't pulled. We'd argued about the house on Evergreen before Theresa arrived.

"If you're open to looking outside of Woodbridge," I said.

Renee cleared her throat again.

"Doing a lot of coughing in there. Do you need water, Renee?" I asked.

"I don't know, Sadie, do I?" she shot back.

Against my better judgment, I pulled up the listing for Evergreen mainly because if I didn't, Renee would keep playing coughing games. "There is one property. It's a little more than your budget, but it meets a lot of what you're looking for." I turned the computer screen so Theresa could see the picture.

"Oh my God, that's perfect looking," Theresa said as the slide show showed the kitchen and master bath suite. "Why didn't you show this to me first? We could have saved a lot of time."

"Unfortunately, we can't see it today."

"Why not?"

"It's… That is, the police have the property cordoned off at the moment. There was an incident this morning near the backyard."

"What kind of incident? Was the property damaged? There aren't hooligans in the neighborhood, are there?"

"Not really." I might as well spit it out and kill her interest then and there. "They found a body this morning."

"What?" Her mouth and eyes both flew open. "You mean like in a murder?"

"Exactly. I didn't mention the property because I figured…"

"Oh my God, an actual murder scene. Christopher's

going to go insane! Maybe he'd be able to help. He's an amateur detective, you know."

It was my turn to widen my eyes. "He is?"

"Oh, yes. Well, not by choice. He's actually a consultant, but crimes seem to happen around him, and he can't help but get involved."

I knew the feeling.

"It's because he cares for people so much," Theresa said. "He has a big heart. When can I see the house? Christopher is going to be so excited when I tell him."

"I'm not sure. I'll have to check with the police."

From her office, Renee shot me a smirk.

"Told you so," she said once Theresa left. I promised to call her about the house as soon as I spoke to Dan Bartlett. "There's a buyer for every property. Even crime scenes."

"Don't gloat yet. She hasn't made an offer."

"She will. The property is gorgeous and she's clearly a crime junkie. She and her partner. Did she say he was an amateur detective?

"Yeah." A consultant who "happened" across crimes. Reminded me of my father's associates—the ones with whom he was currently doing time in a federal prison. Gave me an uneasy feeling. Either that or finding Alex's body this morning was finally catching up to me.

"Since we're talking about the crime scene, I was thinking while you were out," Renee was saying. "I want to stop by Diane's house and pay my respects."

"You do?"

"Don't sound so surprised. I can be sensitive. Considering the circumstances, she can use all the support she can get. The community needs to rally around her."

Unless she was a killer. "That's kind of you, Renee," I said out loud.

"Thank you. I'm going to swing by tonight."

I straightened in my seat. This was the opportunity I needed. "Mind if I join you?"

"You want to see Diane?"

"Sure. Like you said, we should rally around her."

"Won't it be awkward, considering?" She made a rolling gesture with her fingers, referring to my having tripped over Alex's body.

"All the more reason for me to stop by," I said.

"Okay. Let me make a few calls and then we'll head out. We can stop by the market and grab a casserole."

Food. The universal symbol of condolence. "Sounds good." I sat back in my chair. This wouldn't be the first time I hid behind a casserole to get answers.

My number one question: Where was Diane while Alex was taking his late-night trip to Rob's?

10

_____

FOR THE SECOND time in less than a year, I found myself about to offer sympathies to a possible killer.

"You know, I always thought it funny that Tonya and Diane were such good friends," Renee remarked. "They're complete opposites."

"Opposites can't be friends?" *Look at us*, I wanted to say, although we weren't friends so much as super-close acquaintances.

"They can, but these two were super tight. Like bestie sisters or something. The guys were close, too."

Interesting. You'd think a bestie would have mustered up a defense when Jenn called Diane a man-eater. Maybe close proximity had cooled the friendship a little. Or Tonya was a backstabbing bitch of a bestie. It was a fifty-fifty call.

We passed Evergreen Lane. The streetlights were on, and I saw tire tracks in the unplowed snow. I passed the street sign and wondered if Rob was home yet. I'd been texting him all day and the lack of response had me nervous. Especially since Tim had been suspiciously quiet on the subject during our call.

"Looks like we aren't the only ones paying a visit," Renee said as we turned on to Poplar.

I turned my attention to the houses in front of us. The street did seem unusually bright, and I realized it was because every house had front and rear lights on. The Fitzgeralds' oversized colonial was particularly illuminated. Every single room was lit up, including the one over the garage. There was a spotlight in front of the house as well. It shone on a pair of half-melted snowmen in the front yard. Thinking of the one the kids made in Rob's yard, I checked my phone again. Still nothing.

Renee pulled her SUV behind a larger, black SUV with vanity plates. #59.

"The Cooks are here," I said. I wasn't surprised after seeing how friendly Diane and Darius had been yesterday.

There were two more SUVs in the driveway. I recognized the one with the Woodbridge Soccer stickers as Jenn's. The remaining, I assumed, belonged to the Rothsteins. No one in the neighborhood felt like walking after what happened to Alex.

"If there's a crowd, we won't have to worry about making all the small talk," Renee said.

It wasn't small talk I was worried about. It was getting information. How was I supposed to ask questions if there were people around?

Like I suggested, we'd stopped at the local market and purchased a chicken pot pie as a condolence offering. I clutched the shopping bag handles as we picked our way through the frozen footprints in the driveway. I had nearly turned an ankle stepping in a particularly large footprint when Renee stopped—literally—in her tracks.

"Wait a second." Reaching into a bag, she pulled out a business card. "Stick this in with the pie."

I stared at the card. "You've got to be kidding."

"No different than a sympathy card. Only with all my contact information, so she doesn't have to go looking for it if she needs to reach me."

"Should have known you weren't simply being nice." Snatching the card from her fingers, I stuffed it in the bag with the pot pie. "What's next? You going to make me come with you to funerals?"

"Don't be silly. That would be pushy. I send flowers. And only then to select properties."

The au pair, Greta, answered the doorbell. A thick girl with round, muscular shoulders, she smiled at us as she took the pie. "Everyone is bringing so much food," she said in thickly accented English. "It is so nice."

"We tried to pick out something the kids might eat that wasn't macaroni and cheese," I said. "How are they doing?"

Her rosy cheeks lost some of their glow. "All right. They are so young they do not truly understand, I do not think. They keep asking when Mr. Fitzgerald will be home. This morning Mrs. Fitzgerald told them he went on a trip to heaven."

My heart went out to Diane. Keeping a strong front for your children wasn't easy. There were a lot of nights after Jack died when I cried alone in my bed. Even though Tim was in high school and old enough to grieve with me, some feelings could only be released behind closed doors. I couldn't imagine what it would have been like if he'd been a toddler.

"Are they home?" I had to ask. The house was pretty quiet.

"They are watching a movie upstairs with the neighborhood kids. Mrs. Fitzgerald thought it would be a good distraction."

For all of them, no doubt.

Renee cleared her throat. I had a feeling the kid talk was getting to her. "Is Diane here?"

"I'm sorry. She is in the living room with the others. Let me put this down and I will take your coats."

"Who was at the door, Greta? Oh."

Diane came around the hallway and stopped.

I don't know why I was surprised to see Diane looking so put together. Especially since I'd never seen her not put together. She was wearing a long gray cashmere cardigan over a black turtleneck and jeans. A pair of those super-soft designer slippers were on her feet. The only clue that she'd lost her husband was the severe ponytail and slight red around her eyes.

I didn't look like that now, let alone when Jack died. After the funeral, I'd lived in the same Boston sweatshirt and flannel pajama pants for a week until Rob forced me to shower and change.

"Diane!" Renee stepped forward with her arms out, and the two of them clasped manicured hands. "We wanted to stop by to tell you how sorry we were about Alex. It's horrible news. How are you holding up?"

"Best as I can," Diane replied. "It doesn't feel real. I keep thinking he'll walk in the back door and tell me it was all a joke."

"We can hardly believe it ourselves," Renee said.

"The detective who was here this afternoon told me a real estate agent was the one who discovered the body. That wasn't you, was it?"

"No. It was Sadie."

"I'm sorry." Diane's gray eyes slid in my direction for the first time since we'd arrived. I searched for flickers of coldness or something in them that might indicate guilt. All I saw was somber gray fog. "That must have been terrible for you."

"I'm much more concerned about you," I replied. Greta had suddenly moved behind me to take my coat. I slid it off my shoulders and handed it over with a smile that she returned shyly.

"I'll be okay. It's the children I worry about. Alex was such a wonderful father."

But not a wonderful husband? The omission stuck out.

"The others are in the living room," Diane said. Executing a perfect pivot, she motioned for us to follow. "Greta, could you put out cheese and crackers and open another bottle of wine?"

The living room was a great room added on by blowing out the back of their home. French doors and vaulted windows filled the exterior wall, while the interior wall opened like a loft to the landing at the top of the second floor. Diane had done the entire space in chrome, beige, and white oak, creating a space that was bright, but off-putting in its perfection. Kind of like Diane.

I'd been right about the Rothsteins. Tonya sat next to Jenn on a beige leather sofa, while Toshelle Cook perched on the arm, her long legs stretched out in front of her. Again, I was struck by the wardrobe. The three of them could have been attending a Sunday brunch with their skinny jeans and chunky sweaters. Honest to God, didn't anyone in this town dress frumpily anymore?

At least Tonya had the decency to look a little frazzled, but then, she always looked frazzled.

All three held wine glasses.

Meanwhile, Stu and Darius were presenting a study in opposites on the other side of the room. I'd met Stu in passing, but he always struck me as a very full kettle. That is, a guy with so much going on that he didn't need to blow hot air. I liked him. Balding and freckle-faced, he stood at most, five-foot-seven. This afternoon, he looked shorter than that, as he slouched in the nook of the Fitzgeralds' baby grand. He was holding either an ice water or a gin and tonic. My money was on the G&T.

Straddling the bench next to him, Darius looked like a giant. When he saw us walk in, he went to stand up, only to have Diane wave him off.

"Renee and Sadie came by to pay their respects," she said. "Can I get either of you a drink?"

"No, thank you," I said, although part of me could have used one. The atmosphere felt way too weird.

Renee said she'd take a glass of wine and followed Diane through the swinging panel doors into the kitchen to get it. Leaving me to stand in the awkward silence.

"Here, Sadie." Jenn slid over to make room on the sofa. "Have a seat. We were sharing memories about Alex."

"I was talking about the time he and Stu tried to install the garage door opener," Tonya said. "Hooked it to the doorbell by mistake. For a week, the kids kept ringing the doorbell to make the door go up and down."

"Last time I ever tried to install something on my own," Stu said. "There's a reason God invented handymen."

"Alex liked to think he was a handyman," Darius said with a chuckle.

"He helped Brandon with his Scouting project," Jenn chimed in, "since Nick was being a jerk about it."

The others looked at her as though surprised she spoke up. Odd. Usually, Jenn was among the centers of attention.

She flipped her ponytail over her shoulder. "I'm just saying, he seemed pretty handy to me."

"Oh, Alex was always generous when it came to tools. There was nothing he liked better than showing off his drilling prowess."

Tonya's comment must have been an inside joke

because Toshelle gave a soft snort. I looked over at Jenn, and she shrugged.

"Hard to believe we were all together yesterday having a good time." Darius pulled the conversation back from wherever Tonya took it. "Gatherings won't be the same without him."

"No, they won't," Tonya said. "He will be missed."

Stu raised his glass. "To Alex."

"To Alex," the room replied.

While they were taking a sip, I shifted and looked at Tonya. "Renee told me you all were the reason Diane and Alex moved to the neighborhood. I didn't realize."

She nodded. "The six of us have so much in common. We thought it would be nice if Alex and Diane lived closer so we could spend more time together. It was the perfect neighborhood for them. Kid-friendly. Safe…"

Her voice grew thick, and she took another drink.

"I can't believe someone would want to hurt him," Toshelle said.

"None of us do, T." Darius's reply was clipped. "You don't have to keep repeating it."

"I'm trying to process things, *Dar*."

"All of us are," Tonya told her.

"Did you guys see Carmichael leaving with the police this morning?" Stu asked. "Wonder what that was about? You don't suppose he…"

Jenn and I both sat up straighter. "I'm sure it was nothing," she said, saving me the trouble. "Rob wouldn't hurt a fly."

"The police don't drive people downtown without a reason." Stu turned to me. "You were there, Sadie. What's the deal?"

"Um…" Four of the five pairs of eyes were threatening to pin me in place. "Detective Bartlett wanted to ask Rob some questions about a few of the things he saw at the party last night, and with the forensic guys traipsing around the neighborhood, thought it would be easier to talk at the station. And, Jenn's right; Rob wouldn't hurt anyone."

Toshelle had spent the last few moments with her glass raised to her magenta-colored lips, attempting to find any remaining drops. Search done, she proceeded to twirl the stem between her long fingers. "What I'd like to know is what he was doing tromping around outside in the first place," she said. "I thought he was supposed to—"

"He was probably getting some fresh air." Tonya cut her off before she could finish. "He'd been complaining of a headache all night."

"He had? He seemed cheery enough when I saw him," Jenn said.

"Was that before or after he had that fight with Carmichael?" asked Stu. He didn't plan on letting up on Rob anytime soon.

"I'd call it more of a spat than a fight," I quickly corrected. I wasn't letting up either.

"What was more of a spat?"

The swinging door opened, and Diane entered, accompanied by Renee. Behind them, Greta carried a platter of fruit and cheese. Considering the circumstances, it was quite the decorative spread. She set it on the coffee table and disappeared into the kitchen.

Diane pointed to Renee to take a seat in the leather chair before seating herself on the ottoman at her feet. I'd have called the position submissive if it didn't also place Diane in the center of the circle.

"What spat?" she repeated.

"Nothing, Diane," Darius said.

"Stu was talking about the argument Alex had with

Rob Carmichael." Toshelle shot her husband a look as she filled in the details. Clearly, she didn't see the need to be as protective of the widow as her husband. "Whatever Alex said ticked Rob off big time."

"Wonder what it was about?"

I looked at Renee. She had no idea what kind of Pandora's Box her question might open. "People argue about all sorts of things," I said. "Doesn't make it a motive for murder."

"Does if the argument is big enough," Stu said.

"Well, if that's the case, you had words with Alex, too. About money, wasn't it?"

Stu glared at me from over his drink. "Yeah, but I didn't have cops crawling all over my yard this morning."

Diane turned to look at him. "You didn't tell me you and Alex argued about money."

"About that hedge fund he invested in last summer. He wanted to cash out, but the contract has a three-year hold. He didn't like the answer."

"Why did he want to cash out?" I asked.

"I didn't ask," he replied pointedly. A not-so-subtle way of telling me to mind my own business. "Probably wanted to invest in something else."

Or he wanted money to start a new life. I stole a look at Diane. Her expression hadn't changed. Her eyes still looked tired and slightly dazed.

"You know what sucks?" Stu continued. "That was the last conversation we had. I blew him off."

"It's not your fault, babe," Tonya said. "Alex could be prickly sometimes."

"Mercurial," Diane said. "That's what I used to tell him."

She looked at the glass in her hand. "He and I bickered

all weekend. I figured something at work was eating at him."

"Sounds like he argued with a lot of people, and not just Rob," I noted.

"What are you suggesting?"

The question came from Tonya. I'd never realized how harsh her pointed features could look until I saw them drawn into a frown.

"It's all right, Tonya," Diane said. "Sadie's defending her friend. Same thing you'd do for me."

"What I don't get is why he was walking around people's backyards in the first place," Darius said. "That time of night, he should have been…"

"Asleep." Stu finished for him.

"Exactly," Darius said. "Like the rest of us."

"The police asked me the same question," Diane said quietly. "I told them I had no idea. That I didn't hear him leave." Her eyes remained focused on her drink, making it hard to read her expression. I couldn't tell if she was lying or not. Checking around the room, everyone appeared to be looking downward.

"I imagine the police will talk to everyone who was at the party. They do on detective shows," Darius said. He looked in my direction as though I could confirm the theory.

"I'm sure they'll talk to everyone close to Alex. Try to establish a timeline as well as to see if there was anything unusual going on in his life. You know, any red flags." Again, I stole a look in Diane's direction. Her expression still hadn't changed.

"Could we please talk about something else? I'm getting a headache," she asked.

"Sure, Diane. Anything you want. The last thing anyone wants to do is upset you."

"Thank you, Darius." She held out a hand toward him, even though he didn't come close to bridging the space between them. It was more of a symbolic hand-squeeze.

The subtle scent of orange blossom filled the space around me as Jenn leaned in close and whispered in my ear. "I don't care why Alex was at Rob's house. There's no way Rob did anything."

"No kidding," I whispered back.

A movement on the other side of the room caught my attention. The kitchen door. Someone was slowly letting it swing closed. Looked like Greta wasn't above doing a little eavesdropping.

Made me wonder what other things she might have 'overheard.'

11

I TOLD Diane I was getting a glass of water and stepped into the kitchen. The layout was similar to the other kitchens in the neighborhood, U-shaped and opening into a dining area. Greta stood at the island with her back to the door.

She had her arms wrapped around her, and her broad shoulders were shaking.

"Everything all right?" I asked.

She whipped around to reveal tear-filled eyes, which she quickly wiped with her hand. "I—I'm sorry. I was coming to let Mrs. Fitzgerald know I would be heading upstairs when I heard you talking. Is it true? Did…did the police arrest Mr. Carmichael?"

"No one's been arrested yet," I told her. "They had questions, that's all."

"I wish… I mean, why did he have to…." Her lower lip began to quiver, so she trapped it between her teeth to keep it under control. Her fingers played with the bracelet on her wrist.

"Pretty bracelet," I remarked. Reminded me of a

mantra bracelet. It was made of crystal beads the color of tap water, and wrapped around her wrist twice.

The deflection worked. Her lip stilled, and she shook her head. "I'm not sure. It was my mother's. A present from my father when they met. He said it was so she would always remember the day they met. She gave it to me before I left for America."

"So, you can remember her while you were away? That's so sweet."

Poor kid. Probably missed her parents right now. She couldn't be more than nineteen or twenty years old, in the narrow band between teenager and adult. I doubt when she signed up to work in America that having her sponsor found murdered was on her list of potential experiences.

I reached past her to grab a napkin off the counter and handed it to her. "I came in to get a glass of water. Looks like you could use one, too."

"*Danke*. That would be nice."

Diane's modern taste extended to the kitchen. There was lots of chrome and white. I wished her luck keeping it clean when the kids got older. Rounding the island, I started opening cabinets until I found the one with glasses. When I turned, Greta was behind me.

I turned on the faucet. "*Danke*, eh? Are you from Germany?"

"Yes. Just outside of Hamburg."

"I've always wanted to visit Germany." Not really, but it sounded like the proper thing to say. "Woodbridge must feel like a long way from home, then."

"Yes, but I don't mind. I've met some genuinely nice people here."

"In Woodbridge? You'll have to point them out."

She frowned, sarcasm not part of her understanding.

"Never mind," I said as I handed her a glass. She

stared at the contents for a beat or two, then, giving a sniffle, began drinking in dainty, measured sips.

"Mr. Carmichael always treated me nicely," she said, her voice muffled by the rim of the glass.

"I'm not surprised. Rob is a nice guy."

"But the police…"

"The police are doing their job."

The young woman nodded, her pretty blue eyes as wet as the water in her glass. "I don't want them to arrest Mr. Carmichael," she said.

"Neither do I," I replied. "The detective investigating the case is good at his job. I have faith that he'll find the person who did this."

"Do you think so?"

I pictured Dan Bartlett's face. "Positive."

The young woman nodded before looking at her glass. "He was going to help me apply to school here. To take classes so I could become a teacher. Mr. Fitzgerald, I mean."

"That was kind of him."

"He thought I would be good at teaching because I was good with Carter and Natalie." Her lip started quivering again. "Why did Mr. Alex have to go outside?" she whispered. "He was supposed to be here."

Turning to lean against the counter, I pretended to contemplate the grain in the hardwood floor. "Strange how no one noticed he was missing this morning."

"I assumed he was sleeping. He and Mrs. Rothstein said they would be playing until late."

"Playing what?" Tonya didn't mention anything about seeing Alex after the party. What kind of game playing took place late at night?

"Chess," Greta replied when I asked. "When I came to get Carter's *hündchen*—sorry, his toy puppy. I left the toy downstairs. Carter woke up and was upset that his toy wasn't in his bed. Mr. Fitzgerald and Mrs. Rothstein were talking in the kitchen when I walked in."

"What time was this?"

"I am not sure. Ten o'clock or half past, I think. It was after the Rothsteins brought Mrs. Fitzgerald home. I was saying good night to Mr. Fitzgerald when they came in."

"You didn't stay downstairs with them?"

She shook her head as though the idea was crazy. "No. I went upstairs. I only came down again when Carter was crying. I heard them all talking though. Mrs. Rothstein, her voice, it can be heard upstairs."

Especially after a few glasses of wine. "So, you came into the kitchen when Carter started crying," I said, "and Mr. Fitzgerald and Mrs. Rothstein were getting ready to play chess."

"Yes." The au pair nodded. "They told me they would be playing until very late and that I should not worry if I heard them making noise."

I'm sorry, but that was weird. Alex didn't strike me as a chess player, let alone someone to dig out the pieces after a party.

"Did the two of them play chess often?" I asked.

"At least once a week. They have a neighborhood club where they take turns playing against one another. They called it a Robin Tournament?"

"Round Robin."

"That's it." A sad smile tugged the edges of her mouth. "Mr. Fitzgerald used to say that they liked to live life in the fast lane."

A timeline began forming in my head. I already knew Alex left the party early, and that the others left between nine thirty and ten. Then Tonya and Alex decided to play chess around ten thirty. (Don't care if it is a neighborhood thing; it's still weird.) They must not have played though, or they didn't play for long, because Rob said he went for his run at eleven and he would have been gone less than an hour. I made a mental note to ask Tonya.

"Where was Mrs. Fitzgerald during all this?" I asked. "She didn't stay while the others played?"

"I didn't see her in the kitchen. Her wine glass was in the sink. She told the police she had gone to sleep."

Huh. That was also a little weird. If it were me, I'm not sure I'd be comfortable enough to sleep while Jack hung out with another woman. Not that I mistrusted Jack; It would just feel…weird.

You know what else was weird? Greta's answer. I was fairly sure all the bedrooms were on the upper floor. If Greta heard Tonya's voice, then it stood to reason that she would hear Diane as well. Why not say so? "You said you didn't see Diane. Did you hear her when she came upstairs?"

The au pair looked everywhere but at me directly. "She told the police she had gone up," she said, as her fingers fiddled with the bracelet.

"But you didn't hear her?"

Greta's hair spilled forward, forming a blond curtain across her features. There was a soft scraping noise as she slid the glass along the countertop. "No, but why would she lie?"

You tell me, I wanted to ask. It was clear the girl knew something but was struggling with her loyalty to the Fitzgerald family.

"Sometimes people leave out details when talking to the police because they don't think they will make a difference. Like the time they got home, for example." Or burning a blackmail list.

I glanced at the clock. We'd been talking for nearly ten

minutes. Eventually, someone was going to check what was taking me so long. If Greta had any information, I needed to find it out soon.

"Is that what Mrs. Fitzgerald did, Greta?" I tried to keep my voice low and non-threatening as I walked toward her. "Did she tell the police something that didn't sound right?"

Her fingers twisted in the bracelet. "I wasn't there when she spoke to the police."

"You listened though, didn't you?" She shook her head, but the gesture lacked conviction. I set a hand on her shoulder. "It's all right. You won't get in trouble. But if what you know could help us find out who did this to Mr. Fitzgerald... You want to help, don't you?"

"I don't want to get Mrs. Fitzgerald in trouble."

"Greta, I know you care about the Fitzgerald family, but if you know something, you have to tell."

"It's just..." She gave a tiny sniffle. "When I came downstairs with the children this morning, Mrs. Fitzgerald was already up. Her hair was all messy and..."

I waited while she sniffled again. "And?"

She looked at me from over her shoulder, her cheeks pink as pink could be. "She was wearing the same clothes and makeup from last night."

"The pants she wore to the party?"

Greta nodded.

"What the heck, Sadie? Did you decide to dig a well in the backyard?" The door swung open, and Renee sauntered in. "Oh, hello," she said, spying Greta. "Everything okay?"

"Everything is fine," I said. "Greta was a little upset, so I was helping calm her nerves before she went to the children."

"I'm sure today's been pretty traumatic all the way around," Renee remarked.

"Yes, it has," Greta said. To her credit, she blinked back her tears. "My heart aches for the children."

"Poor dears. It's a tragedy all the way around, for sure. An offer just came in for the property on Federal Street. I've got to get to the office and type it up. Are you ready to head out?"

"Actually…" I looked at Greta.

"I should go look in on the children," she said. "The movie they were watching must be nearly over. Thank you for the water."

"Anytime," I replied. "It was nice talking with you."

"It was nice talking with you, too." As she was walking by, she paused. "You won't speak to Mrs. Fitzgerald?" she whispered. "About what I said?"

"Not a word," I replied. To Mrs. Fitzgerald. As for talking with Dan Bartlett?

That was a whole different story.

12

Renee dropped me off in the office parking lot. I waited until she went inside, and then dialed the police station only to learn Detective Bartlett was off duty.

Dammit. Here I was with potentially game-changing information, and no one was around. What happened to working around the clock until the case was solved?

I scrolled through my text log until I found Bartlett's message. The one he sent right after the holidays telling me to let him know if my schedule ever cleared. I'd saved it as a reminder that a man other than my late husband had asked me out.

Learned something interesting about Diane F, I typed. *Care to hear it?* No sooner did I hit send, then I realized I forgot to identify myself. I'd barely typed the first two letters of my name when the phone buzzed in reply.

At Gilroy's. Meet me there.

Guess it didn't matter. I started my car.

GILROY'S TAVERN was Woodbridge's oldest and most townie watering hole. A nighttime Cuppa Joe's, if you will, where people gathered to share gossip over beer and comfort food. The original Gilroy's had been an inn during the Revolutionary War, where minutemen had gathered to share news over beer and comfort food.

This century's version had been furnished by the same decorator as the first one. Low light. Mismatched farmhouse furniture. Early colonial, of course. Pewter plates and mugs hanging on the wall.

The air was thick with the smell of Yankee pot roast when I walked in the door, and my stomach growled in appreciation. In all the day's craziness, I hadn't bothered to eat much. I breathed in the aroma, savored it, and then looked around, steeling myself to see Bartlett.

I found him leaning against the wall behind the vacant hostess stand, reading the local real estate guide. His five o'clock shadow was evidence of his own long day. I told myself he looked tired, not sexy.

"Hey," I greeted and prepared myself for an annoyed glare. After all, I'd been told to mind my own business.

I hadn't steeled myself enough because he looked up, and his blue eyes immediately sucked the air from my lungs. He watched me approach like a hungry man staring down a steak dinner. Probably because he was hungry. We were in a restaurant, after all.

"You don't like to follow directions, do you?" he said when I was close enough.

"Don't have to," I replied. "I have GPS."

"Very funny. Next, you'll tell me I should be grateful you bothered to text at all."

Someone needed to tell him that contrariness was supposed to be sexy. It made looking indignant difficult. "How did you know I was the one who texted?"

"Only a limited number of people would be nosing around for info on Diane."

"Oh."

"Plus, your phone number is on my contact list."

My insides inflated at the news. "I am?"

"Yeah. You're McIntyre's mother. Makes sense I should have his emergency contact info on hand."

"Right." Why else would he save my number? In case I changed my mind about dating him? "At least I know I won't get confused with a telemarketer."

"Depends on what you're selling." Seriously, the man had to tone down the banter before my knees gave out. The hostess returned, and he flashed her a signal indicating two for dinner. "Mind? I missed lunch."

"Not if you don't mind the company," I replied.

"I spend most nights eating in front of the TV. The company's a pleasant bonus."

We followed the hostess through the lounge and into the main dining room, where she directed us to a table for two by the fireplace. This particular setting had a pair of high-back chairs set close together. Very cozy and private. Romantic even.

Gentleman that he was, Bartlett pulled out my chair before taking a seat himself. He loomed large over the small table. Or at least his height and the close quarters made it seem like he did.

I tried to joke away the atmosphere. "Looks like we're finally having dinner," I said, as I arranged my napkin on my lap.

"To think, it only took a dead body and your best friend facing jail to make it happen. If only I'd known earlier. Sorry. Bad joke."

I waved him off. "You forget, I was married to a cop.

Bad jokes come with the territory. Would you mind handing me the wine list? It's been a long day."

"Be my guest."

Our fingers brushed as he handed me the faux leather folder. I'm not sure why I asked for the list in the first place. Wine was Rob's bailiwick. I grew up in a house that paired beer with everything unless it was a special occasion, and then we broke out the sparkling Lambrusco. Sitting in the low light, with Bartlett watching me, however, I felt a need to focus my eyes on something.

"Long day for a lot of people," I corrected as I skimmed the list. "Couldn't have been a picnic for you either. Definitely wasn't a picnic for Rob. Please tell me you let him go home."

"We did."

Thank God. He hadn't been answering my texts and while I'd hoped my friend was simply laying low, there was a kernel of uncertainty that needed Bartlett's confirmation. "How was he?"

"As good as a person who spent the day being interrogated would be. He surrendered his phone, by the way."

That was why he hadn't responded. In retrospect, it made sense. "I thought I'd go by his house tomorrow morning and take him a coffee. Should I pick up some for the surveillance team as well?"

"Very amusing," Bartlett replied. "Just make sure when you go by tomorrow that the two of you don't get into mischief."

I rolled my eyes. "You know, these warnings you and Tim keep doling out are getting old." I was a grown woman, for goodness sake. One who had done and seen quite a bit, thank you very much. Okay, done and seen some. And, mostly in my teens, but that wasn't the point. I knew how to keep my nose clean. "You act like I'm going to go all vigilante justice on people or something."

His look said he wouldn't put it past me. "I'm sure Tim would appreciate not having to bail out his mother."

Fortunately for him, our waitress arrived, preventing my stinging rebuke. Attractive, with a long auburn ponytail, she introduced herself as Lynne and asked if we wanted anything to drink. I ordered a house pinot grigio and waited while he ordered a pot of peppermint tea. His signature drink.

"I would have thought after a day like today, you'd go for a cold one," I remarked. "Jack would have me keep an extra six-pack on hand for exactly that reason. "

"I was more a whiskey guy," Bartlett replied.

"But not anymore?" It was his use of the past tense that prompted me. Wouldn't be the first time someone in law enforcement—or any stressful position for that matter —caught themselves leaning on the bottle more than they should. The fact that Bartlett didn't rush to refute the question gave me my answer.

Instead, he took an extra-long drink from his water glass. When finished, he wiped his lips with the corner of his napkin before smoothing it on his lap.

"Not for five hundred, thirty-two days," he said. "I decided I didn't want to lose my liver."

"Good call." Made me wonder though, what he had lost a year and a half or so ago. He was clearly overqualified for his job in Woodbridge. The house he lived in was a rental full of other people's furniture. The one time I'd visited—while waiting for a tow—I was struck by how few personal items he kept around. Most of the time, I had to tell homeowners to reduce their clutter. I did know he had daughters. Their old school photos were on his mantel. But he'd also told me he hadn't seen them for a while.

Funny, I realized. He'd shown up in Woodbridge with about as much a past as I had.

"Hard to do," I told him. "Quitting something cold turkey. I needed Rob's help in cutting down to one Christmas cookie a day." And even then, it'd been a struggle.

"Sometimes life doesn't give you a choice." For the first time since we'd met, Bartlett's gaze turned distant. I could feel him thinking of the past.

"Life can be harsh that way." Kicking you square in the chest and propelling you into a new life whether you want to move or not. "Still, you succeeded. Not everyone does. Go backbone."

The corner of his mouth twitched. "Backbone?"

"I meant resolve, but I couldn't think of the word fast enough."

At that moment, Lynne returned with our drinks. "I noticed your lantern had gone out," she said, once she finished serving. Reaching into her apron pocket, she pulled out a lighter to relight the candle in the middle of the table. "There you go. Wouldn't want you to strain your eyes reading in the dark."

"Going to need more than a tiny candle to help my eyes," Bartlett replied. "Don't suppose you've got a flash-light I can borrow?"

The woman laughed. "I'll check. We might keep one next to the magnifying glasses."

I had to grab my wine so neither one noticed my jaw drop. Was Bartlett flirting? Not that I cared, but she seemed a little young.

Bartlett waited until Lynne moved on, then raised his teapot. "To resolve," he said, saluting me. "And to backbone."

I took another sip and watched while he fiddled with

his tea, removing the cover from the pot and dunking the bag in the water. Who knew the act of steeping a tea bag could be so elegant?

"I meant what I said last night," I blurted. It caused him to stop mid-dunk. "I'm not purposely trying to avoid you. It's that…"

My lies of omission hung between us. Now was not the time to talk about what I'd done. Who I was. "It's complicated," I settled for saying. "I wish I could explain, but…"

"It's okay," he said.

"No, it's not because I-I really could like you, Dan."

I had no idea where those words came from.

They earned me a semi-smile. "Nice to know."

But he didn't respond in kind. Served me right for pushing him off so long. Good thing I'd saved his text as a memento.

"Well, now that we've cleared the air…" I lifted the menu to hide my face, not because I needed to consider dinner. The pot roast owned me from the second I smelled it.

"What's this interesting tidbit you learned about Diane Fitzgerald?" Bartlett asked.

Right. Diane. The whole point of tracking him down in the first place. I set down the menu and delivered my theory.

"Diane was having an affair."

13

Having made my pronouncement, I backed off. "I mean, I think she's having an affair," I said.

You know how they say eyes can reveal a person's thoughts? Bartlett's eyes had questions. They scrutinized me as he raised his teacup and waited for me to continue. I hated when he looked at me like that, like I'd done something wrong. It wasn't fair. Lynne the waitress got charming. I got Bartlett the Interrogator.

"What makes you think that?" he asked.

"Because she didn't sleep at home last night." Quickly, I relayed what Greta had told me.

Bartlett's cup clattered against the saucer. "You went to see Diane?"

Seriously? I discovered a potentially major clue, and that's what he latches onto, my seeing Diane? "Renee wanted to pay her respects, and I went along to pay mine as well. What's so foolish about that?" I asked.

"And while there, you just happened to chat up the au pair about Diane's whereabouts. I know your MO, McIntyre. You did the same thing when Marylou Paretsky died."

"It's called being polite," I said. "Bringing over a casserole when someone dies is standard operating procedure."

"Even if you barely know the woman and she just happens to be the widow of the man your best friend is suspected of killing? Nice try. That's not being polite, that's snooping."

"Okay, maybe I took advantage of the situation to ask a few questions." So what if I did?

Bartlett leaned closer and dropped his voice a notch. "You were interfering with an active investigation. Which, I might add, you were specifically told not to do."

"I didn't interfere," I retorted. "I offered my condolences. Besides, I ran into Greta by accident. She happened to be in the kitchen when I was getting a glass of water." Close enough. No need to mention my spotting the door being closed.

He made a noise in his throat that sounded a lot like a growl. "I asked you…."

"Do you want to hear what I learned or don't you?"

"Go ahead." Sitting back, he folded his arms across his chest, a position that made his biceps stretch his uniform shirt.

"Like I said, I went into the kitchen to get a glass of water, and Greta was there. We started talking, and naturally, the conversation turned to last night."

"Naturally."

"I didn't go 'Hey that was some murder last night,' if that's what you're thinking. Alex's death was the main thing on everybody's mind. After all, we were there on a condolence call."

"Are we ready to order?" Lynne had returned, this time with a basket of warm rolls which she dropped on the table. "I know you're having the pot roast," she said, pointing her pen at Bartlett.

"What can I say? I'm a creature of habit," Bartlett said. I swear he made his voice sound rougher than usual, turning up the sexy. "Once I find something I like, I stick with it."

"A man who knows what he likes. Nice." Lynne slipped the menu from his hand before turning to me. I ordered the same.

Once she retreated, I helped myself to a roll. "Sounds like you two have had this talk before," I noted dryly.

"You mean about the pot roast? I'm a frequent customer. Beats cooking for one."

Didn't I know it. Sitting at the dining room table with no one across from you could get awfully lonely. Felt weird, thinking of Bartlett as someone who got lonely, but I suppose no one liked spending all their meals by themselves.

Bartlett cleared his throat. I blinked to see him splitting a roll in two. "Getting back to your story," he said. "You went into the kitchen and talked with Greta. What did she have to say?"

I filled him in about Diane wearing last night's clothes.

"Interesting," he said. "But how does that translate to her having an affair?

"Weren't you paying attention? She said she was asleep when Alex left. Clearly, she was lying."

"Or, she could have put on the same clothes when she woke up."

"Suede pants, heels, and a cashmere sweater on a Sunday morning? Before coffee? When she has two small children? No way." Diane might be more together than most women, but even alpha women had their limits. "This was a walk of shame. My guess? She thought she could sneak upstairs and change before anyone woke up, but Greta came downstairs early and blew the plan.

"And…" I added, "if she's cheating, that gives her a reason to want Alex out of the way."

Bartlett reached across the table and picked up the breadbasket. "Are there butter packets in with the rolls?"

What, his friend Lynne didn't provide extra? I fished out a foil-wrapped patty and tossed it in his direction. Oh, for crying out loud. "You have to admit, it's an interesting possibility."

"Interesting, yes, but your theory still has holes."

"Holes?"

"For starters?" He paused while he slathered butter across his roll's fluffy white surface. "Repeating an outfit doesn't prove Diane was having an affair. And…" He held up a finger. "And even if she is, then you've given her an alibi."

"Or a motive," I countered. "If I'm right, it puts her out of the house at the time of the murder."

"Yes, but Alex was dead for a while when you discovered the body. If Diane killed him, why would she wait until early morning to sneak home? Why not go right home so she could shore up her alibi? That's what I'd do."

"Maybe she's not as thorough as you are," I said. The comment earned me a grin. There was another possibility though. "What if she freaked out after the killing and went to her lover's house for help?"

I waited while he chewed on the idea. Actually, he chewed his roll, but I could see him thinking through the idea. "It's possible," he conceded. "People were asleep so they wouldn't necessarily hear a car. Possible, not probable," he added when I grinned. "Still, it's worth looking into."

Still, Bartlett had a point. I chewed on the question along with my roll. "Maybe," I said, thinking out loud, "she freaked out after the deed was done. Panicked and didn't know what to do next. Or…" I had a better thought. "She went to her lover's house to let him know Alex was out of the way. They celebrated for a while, then she came home. Heck, maybe the lover helped her."

"Except both sets of footprints, the one going to Rob's and the one returning were matched to Fitzgerald. How did your killer follow him without leaving a trace?"

Damn. He had me there. "Levitation?"

"Come on, you can do better than that."

There was a glint in his eyes as he finished off his roll. The son-of-a-gun had already figured out the answer and was toying with me.

Challenge accepted. I pictured the crime scene. The snowman with the mismatched gloves, the tracks in the snow from the kids' snowball fight.

Of course! "The killer didn't follow in the snow. She walked along the street to Rob's house. Even if they entered through the sliding patio doors, there were so many footprints that hers would blend in." And then the early morning snow covered the prints further.

"It's a workable theory," Bartlett replied.

One he'd already thought about. "So, you *are* looking into other suspects."

"Didn't I tell you I would, oh ye of little faith?"

Our smiles met. This time I took a minute to admire the way the candlelight brought out the sparkle in his blue eyes. Or maybe that was cockiness. Either way, I had the overwhelming urge to give him a giant hug. I settled for sliding my hand across the table toward his.

"Here you go, two Sunday night specials!"

It was Lynne again, this time with food to accompany her smile. I pulled my hand away just as she set a plate piled high with beef and root vegetables in front of me. Hopefully, no one heard my stomach growl again.

After serving Bartlett's meal, she set a white creamer bowl next to his place. "Remembered the extra gravy this time."

"You are an angel," he replied. "Thank you."

"No sweat. Anything for our regulars," she chirped.

Good God, it was like eating with a sexier version of Rob. I was surprised I didn't have to have Bartlett do my ordering for me so the waitress would hear it.

"Do you need anything else?" Lynne asked. Finally, she looked over at me. "A second glass of wine, ma'am?"

Ma'am? Out of the corner of my eye, I saw Bartlett fighting one of his trademark smirks. Adopting what I liked to call my "Open House" smile—you know, the kind of smile that is aggressively sweet and earnest—I told her I was all set. "I wouldn't want it to mess with my blood pressure medication."

Bartlett lost the battle. A smug smile spread across his face. "Enjoying yourself?" I asked.

"Yes, I am. Surprisingly so," was his answer. The smugness morphed into a gentle amusement that I couldn't help returning.

With our dinners in front of us, eating took precedence over talking. For the next ten minutes, the only sound at the table was of our knives and forks clinking against the plates.

Bartlett was the first to break the silence. "Say Diane did want Alex out of the way so she could be with her mystery lover. There are literally dozens of ways to kill someone. Why stab him with a carving knife at Rob's house?"

"To frame Rob and deflect suspicion away from her." Seemed pretty obvious to me. *Hell hath no fury* and all that. "This way she kills two birds with one stone."

"Only if she knew about their mutual attraction and

Alex's habit of stopping over for late-night talks. If that's the case, then why kill Alex at all? A husband with the hots for his male neighbor makes terrific grounds for divorce."

Especially if he came from a family that valued public opinion and appearance. "Money?" I offered. "She wouldn't get much—anything—in the way of alimony. Maybe she wanted the insurance?"

"Would have to be a pretty big insurance policy." But even as argued the point, he reached behind him for the pocket notebook he kept in his coat pocket. "Making a note for myself. The Fitzgeralds used a Boston-based insurer. We're waiting on them for info."

"Sunday crimes, always a pain," I said, as I pierced a carrot with my fork. "Something Jack used to mutter because so many businesses were closed."

"He's not wrong. Once I get the policy info, I'll have another chat with Diane about the state of her marriage."

Flipping the notebook closed, he returned to his dinner, only to pause before the fork touched his food. "While we're sharing theories, *detective*, was there anything else anything else you learned during 'condolence visit?'"

"Actually, yes," I told him. "Remember the fight Alex had with Stu Rothstein? He said it was about a venture capital investment. Alex wanted to cash out and was mad that he couldn't."

"Stu was at the house, too?"

"They all were. The Cooks, the Rothsteins, Jenn Falcone. The whole gathering was kind of weird."

The notebook flipped open again. "Describe weird."

Thing was, I couldn't. "Nothing specific. It was more of an overall vibe. They were all very focused on Diane."

"That's hardly weird, Sadie. The woman lost her husband."

"I know." And normally, under similar circumstances, I wouldn't bat an eye. "I guess I keep thinking about what Jenn said. About her being the alpha dog."

"You're saying she runs the pack?"

Run? I pictured Diane seated in the center of the gathering, wine in hand and contrasted the image with Rob's party. "I don't know. She's the one who commands the most attention."

"Interesting." He scribbled something down. "I have a meeting with Stu Rothstein in the morning. I don't suppose he elaborated on why Alex wanted his money back."

"No. Just that there was some kind of time lock on the funds."

"A lock-up period. It's designed to keep investors from liquidating early and causing instability. I've read a few investment magazines in my time," he explained. He jotted one final note and closed the notebook, again. "Sounds like you had quite the productive day for someone who wasn't supposed to be poking around."

I stabbed my meat hard enough that tines struck the plate beneath. "If you're giving me a lecture about letting the professionals handle things, I already got two from my son."

"No lecture," Bartlett replied. "We both know you won't listen, so why waste the energy?"

"Thank you." I freed my fork from the beef, and impaled it again, this time more gently. It was nice to know someone understood why I couldn't stand on the sidelines.

"However," he continued, "if you really want to help Rob? Focus on corroborating his alibi. Because right now…"

"It's pretty damn flimsy," I finished for him.

Bartlett's sigh was loud and long. "Flimsy would be a

step up," he said. "The way things stand now; it might as well be nonexistent."

Oh, Rob…

14

DESPITE MY PROTESTS to the contrary, Bartlett paid for dinner. "It's the least I can do since I spent the meal blowing holes in your theory," he said as he handed over his credit card.

I couldn't argue with his logic.

He also insisted on walking me to my car. Hands stuffed in his jacket pocket, he walked slowly beside me, his boot occasionally connecting with one of the loose pebbles mixed with the snow. The atmosphere between us was odd. Simultaneously awkward and comfortably silent. I couldn't help enjoying the feel of his shoulder brushing against mine and wishing we'd met under different circumstances. For the first time in I couldn't remember when I resented my secret. Over the years, I'd become an expert in both ignoring my hidden past and rationalizing the stories I needed to tell for self-protection. Somewhere along the line though, I became a good cop's wife, raised a walking, talking patriotism ad, and developed respect for those who respected the law. It sucked that the quality I liked best about Dan Bartlett—his ethics—was the very thing that prevented me from dating him.

Another stone skittered into the darkness. "You're awfully quiet," he said.

"Sorry. I was thinking."

"I know, I could hear you. Thinking about Rob?"

"Yeah," I said, adding another lie to the pile between us. "Hard to believe it was only last night that we were at his house having a barbecue, and now he's looking at murder charges. Amazing how life can change in the blink of an eye." You'd have thought I'd be used to it, considering my history.

"Tell me about it," he said. "One minute you're cruising along, thinking everything's going great. The next thing you know, life's smacking you on the head."

"Are you speaking from experience?"

"I've had my share of head-whacking, if that's what you're asking. Last one being five hundred and thirty-two days ago," he added.

Oh. Looking over, I saw his gaze focused on the ground. "At least that particular slap had a good outcome."

"Eventually, but not without a price."

His marriage? The one time I'd been in his house, I remembered seeing photographs of his daughters on the mantel. Daughters Bartlett said he didn't see often. I wanted to ask; Bartlett was the one person in Woodbridge who kept his past almost as closed as I did. Problem was, when you started asking someone personal questions, they expected an equal amount of personal information in return, and while I had a prepared backstory, I was uncomfortable sharing fake facts with Bartlett. Silence was easier.

"It's funny," he continued. "When I arrived, I thought for sure I'd landed someplace where nothing ever happened. Last thing I expected was multiple murder cases."

It had been a particularly eventful six months. "People always underestimate the suburbs," I said. "Why did you come here then, if that's what you thought?"

"Because I wanted a town where nothing ever happened."

Ask a stupid question. Breaking the rule I'd made only two minutes earlier, I ventured, "Would it be prying if I asked where you came from?"

"Most recently? Baltimore."

"Pretty city."

"You've been there."

I shook my head. "Saw photos. Jack and Tim were there for a soccer tournament once. It looked nice."

"It can be."

"But not always." I watched the news. I knew.

"Let's say Baltimore is a place where things happen. Too many things."

Like what? I wanted to ask. The bitterness that leaked into his answer made me curious. Wasn't fair to ask his secrets while keeping mine.

"Sorry Woodbridge turned out to be such a hotbed of crime, then."

"I'll live." His accompanying shrug caused his jacket to rub against my arm, and I nearly leaned in closer. "Besides," he said, glancing in my direction. "Woodbridge has its perks."

"Like kickass Yankee pot roast. Don't find that down South."

"No, you don't. You don't find a lot of things."

Dear God, but my cheeks were hot. I hadn't blushed in years, and here I was flushed from head to toe. Naturally, I countered the feeling by tucking my hair behind my ear—because I was eighteen again—and tilting my head away.

"Good to know we didn't scare you away."

"On the contrary. I find myself more and more intrigued."

I tucked my hair again. "Well, we're glad you came to Woodbridge. I mean, the townspeople. All of us. Since we're so crime-ridden and all, that is." I shut my mouth and prayed for a sudden attack of lockjaw. Bartlett, meanwhile, was chuckling. To add insult to injury, the sound made my insides flutter.

"Might as well get your keys out. We're almost to your car." He pointed out my dark SUV two spots away.

Impressive. Without any real estate signs in the back or visible license plate to give it away. "How'd you guess?"

"Recognized the chipped paint on the rear right panel."

I knew the spot. The inch-long result of my banging the roof with a Sale Pending sign the previous summer.

"The shape looks like Connecticut," Bartlett said. "Free association. Works every time."

"Clever. Bet you do some mean party tricks."

"You should see me with moles and freckles. I never forget a birthmark. Careful."

His hand caught my elbow before I could stumble. "Looks like Gilroy's might have to add additional lighting."

Thanks to a series of slip-and-fall claims by drunken customers, Gilroy's had the best-lit parking lot in Massachusetts. Darkness had nothing to do with my fall and everything to do with the way Bartlett decided to lean in when he spoke. The word birthmark was practically murmured in my ear.

"Think you can take it from here?" he asked, hand still on my elbow.

"You mean walk?" Hopefully. "I think so. Last time I looked, I had that skill nearly mastered."

No clue what I said that was funny, but he chuckled again. "I suspect you have plenty of skills mastered, Ms. McIntyre."

I wasn't sure what to say to that. Bartlett's breath filled the silence by tickling my ear.

Suddenly, it disappeared as the grip on my elbow urged me to turn in his direction. Looking up, I saw that his face had sobered. "Look, about Rob," he said. "Thank you for understanding it's not personal."

"You don't spend sixteen years married to a cop and not learn some things." One being they couldn't choose where the clues led. "Not like you planted the evidence in Rob's backyard."

A scowl flickered across his face. Jokes about police misconduct weren't something he found amusing, apparently.

"Don't worry," I reassured him. "I know you're only doing your job."

"Talk to Rob. See if you can prod his memory about last night. Anything he can think of. Anything. Even the stuff he doesn't think matters."

Because even the smallest detail could be important. "Okay," I said.

"If he does remember something, have him call his lawyer. Use proper channels and don't go doing anything...."

"Foolish. So help me, I'm going to scream if I hear that word again."

"Sorry, but there's no guarantee I'll be around to bail you out."

Bail me out? If we weren't standing practically nose to nose, I'd have rolled my eyes and pointed out that I managed a whole lot of decades without him running to my rescue. But the proximity made indignation difficult. There should be a rule that overly presumptive men shouldn't smell like ocean breeze and warm leather. "Twice," I murmured. "You bailed me out twice."

"Well, I'd rather not have to go for three, okay?"

Dammit, if he didn't reach over and curl the hair behind my ears as he spoke. Completely killed whatever little annoyance I might have had left. Instead, I had to settle for lowering my eyes and silently telling my insides to stop melting.

"I'll try," I heard myself whisper.

At least that earned me another spine-warming chuckle. "By the way," he said, finally, finally letting go of my elbow. "I forgot to tell you in the restaurant...."

He leaned down a hair closer. "I like you, too."

15

THE NEXT DAY WAS MONDAY. Normally, that would mean coffee with Rob at Cuppa Joe's. During the week, he and I turned the café into our satellite office. Me catching up on emails and other business, he either preparing for classes or managing his vast fantasy sports empire—usually the latter. In Rob's case, teaching British Literature was a hobby.

His seat was empty, however, when I walked in. I wasn't surprised. News of Alex's murder had hit the news. People would be talking, and while Rob loved being the center of attention, he also liked controlling the reason for the attention. When word got out last fall about his teenage boy band past, he'd been cranky for weeks. The secret clashed horridly with the charming, erudite, British professor persona he'd so carefully crafted.

No wonder we were such good friends. Both of us only let the world see what we wanted it to.

So, maybe you don't know him as well as you thought. You didn't know about Alex...

I shoved the thought away. So maybe, sew buttons. I might not know details, but I knew Rob.

"Sadie?"

I blinked. Rob wasn't there but Jenn was, along with her friend, Erin Koufax, and I was standing in front of their table. The two blondes had come from hot yoga and were dressed in leggings and oversized sweaters. "You look a little dazed," Jenn said. "We thought maybe you heard bad news."

"Or were stoned," Erin added. She flicked off her coffee lid with her thumb.

I ignored the jibe. She was still annoyed over her secret marijuana business getting closed down.

"Just thinking what to order," I said. "I've been in a midwinter latte rut."

"Oh, good," she replied. "I was afraid you'd heard something about Rob. Have you heard from him? He didn't answer my text."

"Last night." *Finally.* "Said he was worn out, and we would talk later."

"When you do, will you let him know I'm thinking of him? I'm taking over chocolate chip cookies later."

Ha! Take that, Bartlett. I told him delivering food during a time of crisis was the suburban way. Some of us simply chose to deliver it strategically.

"I'm sure he'll appreciate it," I said.

"It's the least I can do. We don't believe for a minute that he had anything to do with Alex's murder. Right, Erin?"

Erin shrugged enthusiastically. "He lied about being in a boy band."

"And you lied about having a marijuana farm in your basement," I reminded her. "So what?"

"Means I know what I'm talking about. People will lie about anything to save themselves."

I bristled at the remark. "Not everyone. Especially Rob."

"Stu Rothstein disagrees."

Stu? When did Erin talk with Stu?

Jenn flipped her ponytail off her shoulder. "He was in here earlier, spouting off while waiting for his coffee. Same stuff as yesterday, about how Rob's argument with Alex was super suspicious."

"You don't think so?" Erin asked.

She waved a hand. "That group doesn't like anyone outside their little coalition. Sorry," she said upon seeing Erin's and my blank looks. "A coalition is a group of chee-tahs. Brandon's going through a nature phase. We've been watching a lot of animal programs. Now my brain is filled with useless trivia. Like a group of cats is called a clowder."

"What would you call a group of weasels?" Erin sneered in my direction as she asked. I sneered back.

"A colony," Jenn replied. "Or a pack, which now that I think of it, is a much better word choice. Coalition is more fun to say, though."

She could call them anything she wanted; I was more interested in the other part of her sentence. I grabbed a chair from the next table and sat. "What do you mean, they don't like anyone outside the group?"

"You saw them yesterday, all cliquey, with their little inside jokes. It's like the six of them are joined at the hips."

"Five now." As usual, Erin was helpful by pointing out the obvious.

"Fine, five. It used to be six. Anyway, the whole neigh-borhood talks about it. The six of them are always doing stuff together and never including anyone else."

"Towns like Woodbridge are full of cliques," I said. Six months ago, people were saying the same thing about Jen,

Erin, and their friends, until one of them turned out to be a killer.

"This is way more than a clique, Sadie. It's like a...I don't know what, but it's weird. They are way too into each other's lives. Like they can't do anything with anyone who isn't part of their group."

"You're just mad because they stopped inviting you to the barbecues. I helped her make the brownies for one," Erin said.

"Puh-leeze. If they're going to be that thin-skinned about things, I don't want to go to their stupid parties anyway."

Based on the vehemence of her denial, I would beg to differ. "What happened? Didn't they appreciate the secret ingredient?"

"No. They loved the brownies. Gobbled them right up. It's not my fault I was on antibiotics and didn't want to have any."

"I told you, Jenn, having an edible isn't the same as drinking alcohol..."

"Excuse me, Erin, for not wanting to take a chance and have to take another round. You can become resistant, you know. They didn't have to act like it was this huge offense."

"What was a huge offense?" I asked.

"Not eating the brownies."

"Are you saying they stopped inviting you because you didn't feel like getting stoned?"

"No, because I wouldn't eat dessert, period."

I frowned. "That makes zero sense. Why would they care if you didn't eat dessert?"

"I know, right? Who gets bent out of shape over healthy eating?"

"I still think Nick talked trash about you to them," Erin

said. Nick, being Jenn's ex-husband. "Sounds like something he would do."

"Then why not say something?" Jenn asked. "Or do what the rest of us do when we don't want to invite someone and blame the slight on a miscommunication? Why make up some lame excuse about not liking dessert as much as they do?"

"Seriously," she said, giving her ponytail another flip. My skepticism must have shown on my face. "Diane said it straight up."

"She told you they didn't want to hang out because you didn't eat brownies."

Jenn cleared her throat and mimicked Diane's imperious tone. "We adore you, Jennifer, but it's clear from the way you continually turn down dessert that we don't share the same tastes."

Certainly sounded like something Diane would say. But why? "Are you sure it was about dessert?"

"It was the only thing I refused," she replied. "You know what the weird thing is? The first time I went to one of their parties, they were thrilled to see me. Darius rubbed my shoulders after I mentioned I'd been driving all day."

"Oh, really?" Erin said. She and I exchanged a look. We might not like each other, but our minds worked in similar ways, and in this case, a picture was beginning to form. Jenn was a beautiful woman.

"What do you mean, by 'oh, really?'" Jenn asked.

"If you ask me, I'm guessing Toshelle didn't like her husband paying attention to the new neighborhood divorcée," Erin said.

"What? No way."

Or someone didn't, I added to myself. "Were you flirting?" Jenn was second only to Rob in that department.

"I was being myself."

Meaning yes. Maybe not on purpose—I had a feeling flirting was a conditioned response when it came to Jenn—but that didn't mean it wasn't annoying.

"And he was giving everyone shoulder rubs," Jenn continued. "Stu and Alex were, too."

Only not everyone in the group was a stunning, recently single blonde.

I could see Toshelle getting annoyed. Tonya and Diane too. Diane, especially, if she felt her man-eater status was threatened.

"Face it, Jenn," Erin said. "You got iced out by the other wives."

I nodded.

Jenn looked at us both before giving a dismissive sniff. "Well, I still say they're weird. And that they take their desserts way too seriously. Every time I turned around, they were pushing it on me. *Ready for dessert, Jenn? Looking forward to dessert, Jenn?* Hello? Some of us want to fit into our pants."

She took a sip of coffee. "Do you really think I got wife-blocked?"

"Makes a lot more sense than being blackballed because you wouldn't eat the brownies." I frowned. "You're right, that is a lame excuse."

"Stupid too. Like I'd be interested in any of them. Well, maybe Stu. What?" she asked when Erin laughed. "Have you ever heard him talk business? Brainy finance guys are hot. Besides, I already did the super-cool jock route with Nick. Look where that got me."

Speaking of bad marriages... "You haven't heard anything about the Fitzgeralds' marriage, have you?" I asked Jenn.

"Like what?"

"Like if they were having problems? If one of them had someone on the side?"

"Well… Alex did spend a lot of time with the kids and the au pair, but everyone in the neighborhood figured it was because he was the one who wanted them more. Honestly, I think he'd be afraid to cheat on Diane."

"And Diane?" That's what I wanted to know.

Jenn shrugged. "When would she have the time? She's either at work, with the kids, or with the coalition."

Not to mention playing in the neighborhood chess club. Quite a busy neighborhood.

"Maybe she's a good multi-tasker," Erin said, "and tossing him in at lunch."

"If she is, she needs to share her secret, because I'd be too freaking tired," Jenn replied. "Hell, I was too tired to sleep with my actual husband, when I had one."

"You also couldn't stand your actual husband," Erin pointed out.

"I did, at one point."

While the two of them debated Diane Fitzgerald's sexual time management skills, I went over Jenn's story. Late-night games, exclusionary dinners. They were an incestuous little group.

I couldn't imagine the others would be happy if they discovered Alex was considering breaking away.

Could one of them be upset enough for murder?

The alarm on my cell phone went off. Damn, I had an appointment with Theresa.

"I have to go," I announced. "I've got a client who's interested in the Wiggins house."

The news of a potential neighbor made Jenn sit up straighter. "Even with the dead body? What's their name? More importantly, do they have sons who like nature programs?"

"Her name is Theresa Crowe. I don't believe she and her partner have children, and apparently knowing there was a murder nearby doesn't faze her." I checked the time on my phone screen. "I'm going to be late if I don't hustle. I'll let Rob know about the cookies."

Jenn was too busy frowning at her coffee cup to reply. "Funny," she said.

"What is?" I asked.

"You're showing a murder house to Mrs. Crowe," she said. "A group of crows is called a murder. Kinda apropos, don't you think?"

16

"As you can see, the kitchen is brand new. You've got a double wall oven as well as a range top with an indoor grill. Keeps you from having to shovel a path if you want to grill a steak in January." I smiled at Theresa, who was busy scribbling notes in a small leather notebook, a la Dan Bartlett, only Bartlett didn't keep the three-by-five pad directly in front of his nose.

"Christopher and I are vegetarians," she said, without glancing up.

"Well, now you can grill vegetables year-round," I chirped. If my voice got any sunnier, I would need sunglasses.

"Uh-huh." Theresa kept scribbling. "The previous owners, the Wiggins's, you said they knew the man who died in their yard?"

Her question pretty much encapsulated the appointment. While I pointed out every possible amenity, Theresa asked questions about Alex's murder. "I want to make sure I capture as much information as possible for Christopher," she'd said when we started. Silly me thought she meant room dimensions.

Theresa was waiting for me to answer her question. "Hard to say. The Fitzgeralds live one street over. But this is a friendly neighborhood, so I wouldn't be surprised if they at least spoke to one another."

"Hmmm." After a bit more scribbling, she walked around the room, opening and closing the cupboards while I hung near the door. With the memory of seeing Alex's leg through the kitchen window still fresh in my mind, I was in no mood to move any closer. I was already dreading the inevitable request to visit the taped-off area. That Theresa didn't rush straight to the backyard upon pulling up was a minor miracle.

"Maple?"

"Um, oak I think." Hearing an actual question about the house threw me for a second. "I can check if it makes a difference."

"Not really, so long as it's a hard wood. Softer woods scratch terribly. Christopher once broke open a missing person's case through the scratches left on a pine door, you know. He's always finding minute details like that, things others miss. The way his brain works..." She clutched at her bosom. "His brilliance never ceases to amaze me."

Funny that I'd never heard of him. "I'm surprised the town paper hasn't done a write-up," I said. A town resident who was a police consultant was a topic tailor-made for a local newspaper. Our local editor, Jessica Dembrowski, tried to interview me five times after the whole Marylou thing.

"He's much too modest for any kind of personal promotion. He'd much rather keep his involvement under the radar and let the police receive credit. Most of the time his involvement is reluctant, anyway."

Crimes fell into his lap, was how she described it on Sunday, or something close to that. "He sounds like a fascinating man," I said. Actually, he sounded like something out of a comic book. Even so, I found myself intrigued by this modest, brilliant crime fighter. "What does he do when he's not working for the police?"

"He's a professor of psychology," Theresa replied. "He specializes in criminal behavior."

No wonder the police called on him.

Having finished examining the cupboards, Theresa moved toward the kitchen window. I braced myself. As soon as I heard her gasp, I knew what was coming.

"You can see the crime scene from this window!" She rose on tiptoes to get a better view. Without drawing closer, I knew what she was seeing. Snow tracked with footprints and broken branches from where Alex stumbled to his final resting place. Yellow police tape still marked off the area from where Alex fell to where his walk began, in Rob's backyard.

"Christopher is going to be so excited. I must take some photographs. How do we get outside?"

"I wouldn't get too close," I said, pointing to the door. "I'm not sure if the police are finished with their analysis."

Her lips formed a tight, thin line. "I know how a crime scene works. I've been with Christopher for nearly seven years."

"Sorry. Force of habit," I replied, before adding, "My late husband was a police officer."

Immediately, her face shifted from annoyance to an expression of comradery. "I understand completely," she said. "Our investigative men train us well, don't they? Are you coming?"

I hesitated, feeling queasy at the idea. This wasn't my

first crime scene, mind you, but it was the first familiar dead body I'd seen since my previous life.

Still, I was going to have to look at the yard eventually, either while showing the house or at the home inspection. I might as well start now. "Sure."

We stepped out onto the deck. The Wiggins's backyard was a crisscrossed trail of footprints and wheel marks. Despite this, I could still make out my footprints from Sunday. I followed them again, grateful that this time I'd thought to wear boots.

"Alex's body was behind the shed," I told her. I didn't have to tell her he cut through the backyards before collapsing. It was obvious from the tape.

Theresa didn't need me to tell her either. Her eyes followed the tape leftward before pulling out her cell phone and snapping photographs of the trampled ground where Alex had lain. The spots where the blood had dripped into the snow had turned a mottled brown. Theresa snapped shots from several angles.

"The victim was stabbed, correct?" she asked.

"Once. In the chest." I answered automatically, only realizing my slip after the words left my mouth.

Theresa picked up on it instantly. "How do you know that? It wasn't in the news accounts."

Might as well go with the truth. "Because I'm the one who found the body," I told her.

"Oh my gosh, did you? How?" She flipped a page in her notebook, her eyes glistening with excitement. "You have to tell me everything," she said.

Everything was a tall order. I told her what I could, making sure to leave out anything that happened once the police arrived.

Theresa wrote down every word. "This is absolutely

marvelous. And you knew the victim too, right? You mentioned their last name and where they lived."

Well played, Theresa. She was sharper than I gave her credit. "Tangentially," I said. "Our paths crossed occasionally."

"It must have been traumatic for you. Stumbling upon the dead body of a friend."

"Acquaintance," I corrected, "and I've had more pleasant experiences. Why don't we go inside?"

The longer she was here, the more likely she was to ask about the rest of the crime scene. The fewer people who knew about the snowman in Rob's yard, the better. "I didn't get the chance to show you all the amenities in the bathrooms. Did you notice there was a bidet in the ensuite bathroom?"

"There's no need. I've seen everything I need to see."

My shoulders sagged as I watched her take another photo. So much for selling the house. I thought this sale was in the bag, but it appeared central air and a furnished basement weren't as appealing as the crime scene.

"Very good then," I said. "Let me lock up, and I'll take you to the office so you can retrieve your car." I turned to make the long walk through the snow to the kitchen door.

"I did have one more question," Theresa said. "Is there a lot of foot traffic?"

"Foot traffic?"

"You know. People going back and forth at all hours. Walkers, runners, bicyclists."

Why? Did she think there might be a witness? "Very little," I said. "This is a cul-de-sac so by nature it's a quiet street."

"The street we live on now has much too much foot traffic. Benito, poor little thing, gets worked up every time. Christopher and I prefer peace and quiet." The woman looked over her shoulder at Alex's final resting spot. "Ask them if they'll take fifteen thousand less."

"You…?" Took me a minute to realize we were back to discussing the property. "You want the house?"

"Of course I do; it's absolutely perfect. As long as you're certain Benito won't be bothered."

I hadn't the slightest idea, so I did the next best thing. I pretended I was Renee and skirted the issue. "I'm certain Benito will love living here. The yard is perfect for a dog."

"Wonderful. Christopher will be thrilled."

Christopher wasn't the only one. Now if I could have the same kind of luck clearing Rob's name.

I wondered if Christopher hired out on a private basis. We could use him.

17

"So NOT ONLY DID SHE put an offer on the house, but once she found out that my son was also on the police force, she became my best friend. She even invited me to join her and her partner for tea. I figured you could come, too."

I waited for the man on the other side of the breakfast bar to respond. With his head propped by one hand, Rob stared at the countertop as though the patterns in the marble held the secret to life.

Throughout our friendship, I'd seen Rob in a variety of states: sick, hungover, brokenhearted, and bouncy as a puppy on new grass. Never though, had I seen him like this. He wasn't simply down; he was lifeless. His eyes were flat and I could feel his despair every time he let out a deep breath.

It wasn't right. This was Rob Carmichael, Mr. Magnetic North himself, to whom all things living were attracted. He was supposed to exude light and energy. To see him this way broke my heart.

I reached over and brushed the cookie crumbs off his

T-shirt. "It's a truly bad day when one of my crazy client stories can't distract you," I said.

"Yesterday was a bad day," he said. "Today is reality sinking in. A man I cared about was stabbed in me kitchen, and I'm being blamed." I noticed the poshness had slipped from his voice. His native Manchester accent always kicked in when he was stressed.

"Only because Dan Bartlett hasn't found the real killer yet. Trust the process," I said, echoing Bartlett's advice to me.

He looked at me with sunken eyes. "Is this the same Dan Bartlett who kept me in a room for six bloody hours going over the same details? Who, when he let me go, told me I should retain a lawyer? A *good* lawyer, he said. I'm supposed to trust he's looking for someone else?"

"Yes, you are," I told him. I've only known Bartlett for a few months, but I know he's one of the good guys. Cops like Bartlett, and my Jack, for that matter, were like Boy Scouts with a badge. They believed in things like justice and honesty.

"He said he would look at every angle, and I believe him. In fact, he and I ran through alternative theories last night."

That perked him up. "We?"

"I may or may not have shared some information I discovered with him over pot roast." I headed to the stove to turn on the kettle, helping myself to one of Jenn's cookies on the way. With my free hand, I took a pair of mugs from the cabinet along with the tin of Rose Pouchong tea, Rob's current favorite blend.

"Did you think I was going to sit around and not do some digging?" I asked. "What kind of best friend would that make me?"

"Probably normal," Rob replied, with a glimmer of his old cheek. "Did you find out anything?"

"As a matter of fact, I did. Turns out—Dear God, these cookies are amazing!" Was that toffee I tasted mixed in with the chocolate? How could Jenn bake cookies like this and then not like to eat dessert? It boggled the mind. I shoved the rest of the cookie in my mouth and grabbed another.

In between bites, I told Rob about Diane wearing the same clothes on Sunday morning.

"Suede pants at dawn? I know Diane likes to look Instagram-ready ready but being that dressed up on a Sunday morning seems out of character, even for her," he said.

"Unless she didn't sleep at home."

"Meaning what? She's stepping out?" Lines appeared on his forehead as he thought through the idea. "I suppose she could be, but how does that help me? If anything, doesn't that give Diane an alibi?"

Bartlett said the same thing, but I still thought it was an important piece of the puzzle. Diane had the most to gain from Alex's death.

"Do you think there's a chance Alex found out, and that was why he was eager to talk with you?"

"Maybe," he replied. "Or maybe he wanted to run off together and join the circus. We'll never know."

I watched as the small spark I saw earlier had flamed out, replaced by downcast eyes. His index finger traced invisible patterns on the countertop. "Hey!" I said, stilling his hand. "You can talk to me, you know. I've been there. Having someone you care about taken away without warning, that is."

A hint of a smile tugged at his mouth. "I know. I'm not sure if I'm ready yet, though."

I understood that, too.

The kettle whistled. I poured us each a cup of tea and pushed one toward him along with the plate of Jenn's cookies. Experience taught me that grief was easier to cope with when paired with baked goods. A book of poetry lay on the counter, not far from the plate. *Ariel.* "You're reading Sylvia Plath?" I said. Considering the circumstances, depressing poetry didn't seem like a good idea.

"The Fitzgerald au pair brought it over to me."

"Greta came over?"

"Around ten o'clock. She said she found the book in a box of old books at the house and thought I might enjoy it. Said it was one of her mother's favorite books. Sweet kid. I didn't have the heart to tell her I'm not a fan of Plath's work. Especially after she helped me clean up."

I had to agree on the sweet assessment. "For what it's worth, she doesn't think you had anything to do with Alex's death, either. She told me how you'd always been nice to her."

"I feel bad for her. Diane's a hard employer to please. Plus told me she likes listening to Be-bop-alicious."

"You're kidding. She does?"

"I know, right? If I weren't so bloody tired, I might have felt guilty for letting her bleach the kitchen floor."

For the next five minutes, we drank our tea, the only noise in the chirping of birds outside. Sometimes having someone close by helped.

"I liked him," Rob said suddenly. "I mean, I think I could have *really* liked him if he'd been available."

His fingers played with the string on his teabag, twisting and untwisting it around his knuckle. "Been a long time since I clicked with someone the way we clicked. I tried to tell myself the sparks were in my head."

"Except they weren't."

He let the string slip from his finger. "Oh well, probably wouldn't have worked even if he had left Diane."

"Why not?" I recognized rationalization when I heard it. He was trying to minimize what happened between them, as though that might minimize the hurt as well.

"I would always be the person who broke up his family. That was his biggest fear, you know. Diane keeping his kids away from him."

"Do you think she knew about you two?"

"If she did, Alex wasn't aware of it. Honestly, Sadie, the guy was so far in the closet, it took him thirty-eight years to know himself. I don't see how anyone else knew."

Leaving Rob to steep his tea, I grabbed another cookie and walked to the patio door. Like the Wiggins's backyard, Rob's yard had also been reduced to a crisscrossed mess of litter and footprints. Some impressions had been reduced to slush, with brown patches of grass visible beneath their translucent surface. Saturday's snowman stood in the middle of the tracks, the left side of its midsection smeared with brown from its wound. I stared at the stain.

"Why did he stab the snowman?" I wondered out loud. "Hurt and in pain, why would he spend his energy jamming the weapon into the snow when he could drop it on the ground? Think he was trying to tell us something?"

"The man had a knife stuck in his chest. Doubt he was thinking about anything, at least not logically."

My gut wasn't so sure. Of course, when you're desperate for answers, you start looking for meaning in everything, too, and for Rob's sake, I was feeling desperate.

"Did Alex ever mention anything about a neighborhood chess club?" I asked.

"No. Why?"

"Greta told me that Alex and Tonya Rothstein stayed

up playing chess on Saturday night. They were part of a neighborhood club of some kind."

His features drew into a frown. "First time I've heard of it, but I wouldn't be surprised. He used to joke that his street had a bit of a co-dependent thing going on."

Interesting. "Jenn said the same thing. She called them a coalition—that's a group of cheetahs, but the way."

"I know. Jenn visited, remember? She's right, too. The six of them were always in and out of each other's houses. Alex said he was getting tired of it. God, I wish I'd stayed inside Saturday night." Tea sloshed onto the marble as he shoved the mug aside.

"You didn't know he was coming over," I said.

"I suspected. Alex said he needed to talk to me. Kept trying to catch my eye all night. I didn't want to deal with him."

I was across the room in a flash, unable to stand hearing the guilt in Rob's voice. Before I could finish wrapping my arms around him, he was pressed against me, arms squeezing my shoulders.

What a lot of people don't realize about Rob is that while he seems blasé and happy-go-lucky, he has a deeply sensitive soul. The guilt from not saving Alex will haunt him for a long time. Didn't matter who held the knife.

"There now," I whispered as his shoulders began to shake. "Everything is going to be all right." I ran my hand along his spine, like you would to soothe a child.

After a few minutes, the shaking subsided and Rob lifted his head, showing his damp eyes. He hadn't so much cried as he'd choked back tears. "What am I going to do?" he asked. "I can't go to his funeral because the whole town thinks I killed him."

"Not the whole town," I reminded him. "You still have me. Not to mention Tim and Jenn and Carlos at Cuppas."

And Dan Bartlett, though if asked, he'd claim neutrality. "Believe me. There are a lot of people who believe in your innocence."

"Thanks." He sniffed back his emotions. "Means a lot, you standing by me. At least I'll have someone to see on Visitor's Day."

"You're not going to prison. I promise."

"Exactly how do you plan to keep that promise, luv? Go on the run with me? Knock Bartlett on the head and help me escape while he's unconscious?"

"Don't be ridiculous. We're going to find someone to confirm your alibi."

"We'd be better off going on the run," Rob said. He ran his fingers through his hair, making the already mussed-up locks even messier looking. The look was attractive, damn him. "I've replayed Saturday night at least a dozen times and nothing comes to mind. I saw no one."

"What about your fitness tracker? Doesn't that list activity by the hour?"

"It would have, if I'd worn it. I sent it in for repairs last week. Face it, Sadie, I'm screwed." Letting out a groan, he collapsed on a stool and buried his face in his hands.

I looked at my best friend's slumped shoulders. One thing was certain, sitting around his kitchen eating chocolate chip cookies wouldn't help. "That's it, mister," I told him. "No more self-pity. You can beat this. How many times did you tell me how you pulled yourself out of poverty to earn your graduate degree?"

"Because I was good-looking and could carry a tune. Don't see how either's going to help me much now."

"They aren't," I said. Well, his face might—I would never underestimate the power of Rob's face. "But tenacity will."

Outside, shadows appeared on the snow. It was getting

dark. Too late to put any plan into motion. Tomorrow, however, was a different story. "I'm going to pick you up at nine a.m.," I said. "Be dressed and ready to go."

"Why? Where are we going?"

"To find you an alibi, of course. We're going to clear your name if it's the last thing we do."

18

My CELL PHONE rang as soon as I pulled into my driveway. I answered on the second ring. "This is Sadie," I chirped. "Hello?"

Nothing but silence greeted me.

"Hello? Is anyone there?"

The caller hung up.

A wrong number. Or a robocall. They were a plague upon the nation. I checked the call screen to make sure.

The number had a New Jersey area code.

It was a coincidence, that's all. A lot of people lived in New Jersey. Lots of reasons why someone from that area code might call and hang up. Perfectly logical reasons that had nothing to do with me.

I hurried into the house and programmed the alarm system, just in case. If anyone came by, my doorbell camera would spot them. Then, I grabbed my laptop and sat on the floor, pretzel-style. I hadn't removed my coat, but that was all right. If I had to run, I would need it anyway, along with my emergency exit bag that was stashed in my closet. Hopefully, the clothes still fit.

My fingers trembled as I typed in the address for the Prisons and Prisoners website, the government's database of federal inmates. The statuses for Carmine Albano and Dougie Girardi remained unchanged. Incarcerated.

Thank goodness. I let out a long, shaky breath. I hadn't had a scare like that in a couple of years. That's one of the problems with being in WITSEC. The government might give you a new identity and a new life, but it can't erase your old life from your brain. You never completely forget, no matter how many years go by. For me, I remembered every time Tim laughed or cocked his head a certain way. The memory terrified me to death. If my father or Dougie ever found out about Tim, or if Tim were to find out about them... I shuddered to think about it.

Fortunately, I didn't have to tonight.

19
___

"All right, what's the plan?" Rob asked. He was dressed and waiting for me in the kitchen, his cat Eliot sitting on his lap.

"We walk," I replied, "and we stuff these in people's mailboxes." I handed him one of the flyers I'd designed the night before.

"Camera footage?"

"Yep. From every house on your running route that has one of those home nesting cameras or a doorbell camera."

The idea came to me following last night's scare. We'd flood the neighborhood with flyers asking residents who had cameras to contact Rob's lawyer.

"If the cameras are angled like mine, then they have a partial street view. One of them is bound to have caught you on camera, even if only your sneakers." The bright orange Sauconys were easily recognizable, especially as Rob tended to wear reflective-trimmed compression pants with them.

He didn't look convinced.

"I know it's not the most sophisticated plan," I told

him, "but Jack used to say that sometimes the best evidence is found by unsophisticated methods. It's worth a shot, isn't it? Beats sitting home and waiting for news, doesn't it?"

We bundled up and headed out. Thankfully, it was a sunny day, so walking wouldn't be too horrible. I say *too* because Rob's route was eight miles.

"I hope you know I wouldn't walk eight miles in the middle of the winter for just anyone," I told him as we moved along. "In fact, it's a limited list. You and Tim."

"I'm honored to have made the cut."

"You should be."

Suddenly, Rob jumped in front of me to block my path. "I mean it, Sadie," he said, looking me in the eye. "You have no idea how much I appreciate what you're doing. Not just this…" He gestured at the flyers, "but everything. For yesterday. I was…"

"Forget it," I said. "You'd do the same for me."

"Maybe. If I wasn't busy or something."

Now that was the Rob I knew. Smiling, I smacked his shoulder. "Turn and get going. We've got a lot of houses to cover."

———

"I WAS WONDERING…" Rob said.

It was an hour later. By this point, Rob and I had covered much of his route. We considered knocking on every door, but in Woodbridge, strangers knocking on doors were always deemed suspicious, so we settled for stuffing flyers in mailboxes, and since most mailboxes were on posts in front of the house, distribution went fast. We did manage to spy on a couple of houses whose doorbell cameras were visible from the street. In those instances, we rang the bell, hoping to speak to a live person, but no such luck. I wrote down the addresses so we could call later.

"Why, in a town where residents pay attention to every little activity on their street, there aren't more people with home security systems?" I would have thought multiple houses in Rob's neighborhood would have them. Was I the only one in town who worried about strangers appearing on my doorstep?

"Sorry," I quickly added. "I don't mean to sound discouraging. I'm sure you'll show up on the footage from the ones we did find."

He rubbed his gloved hands together. "No worries, luv. Strangely enough, I'm feeling encouraged. I didn't think we'd find any cameras, and here we are with four real possibilities. It's more hope than I've had all week."

"Good." If our hunting expedition didn't do anything more than lift Rob's spirits for a few hours, it was a partial success. "What were you wondering then?"

"What if Alex didn't know his attacker? We're assuming the killer was someone from his circle, but what if it was random? Like a burglar or…."

"Someone after you?"

His blue eyes widened. "Who would want to hurt me?"

Good point. Someone would have to dislike Rob to want to hurt him. A burglar, though, seemed a reach. "I suppose it's possible that Rob interrupted someone breaking into the house, but the lights were on. Wouldn't it make more sense for someone to break into a house that was dark?"

"Maybe they saw me leave and thought the house was empty."

"I don't know." If it was a random stranger, they would be harder to find. Especially if they were wearing gloves so as not to leave fingerprints. "I suppose it's plausible, but in general, most victims know their killers."

"I know." He sighed, before rubbing his hands again. "I guess I'm hoping the killer won't be a neighbor. We already went through all that business with Marylou's murder."

"Says something about our sleepy little town, doesn't it?" I thought of what Bartlett said. About how he came to Woodbridge because he thought nothing ever happened here and how wrong he'd been.

"Yeah, like *Don't Move Here*."

I bopped him on the head with the rolled-up flyers. "Hush your mouth. If Renee hears you say that, she'll have you evicted. And," I lifted my finger, "don't tell me a person can't be evicted from a town. If there's a way to do it, Renee will. Why do you keep rubbing your hands?" He was doing it again while we talked.

"Because I'm cold! Bloody driving gloves are too thin. I lost my woolen ones somewhere. I swear I lose at least three pairs a season."

"Do you want to borrow mine?" I asked.

"And then feel guilty watching you trying to warm your fingers? No, thank you. We've only got a short while left, anyway. Auburndale Street is the next right. I ran down it as far as the stop sign, then turned around."

Auburndale Street lined the town cemetery. One of the town cemeteries, that is. Woodbridge had two cemeteries. There was the modern cemetery on the outskirts of town, where Jack was buried, and this one, with stones dating to the eighteenth century. A tall iron fence surrounded the property, ostensibly to stop vandalism, but based on the number of toppled headstones, it wasn't entirely effective.

Most of the houses on this street were older as well. Victorians that had been refurbished. The kind of home popular with young couples looking for an affordable way of buying into Woodbridge's stellar amenities. A few of the houses had been converted into luxury apartments. The people who lived there tended to be older with incomes decent enough to afford the (inflated, in my opinion) rent. My gut said these rentals would be a good bet for security systems.

"For some reason," I said as I closed a mailbox's front flap, "the name Auburndale Street sounds familiar."

"You're a Realtor. Wouldn't all streets sound familiar?"

"Not necessarily." This was different. Someone mentioned Auburndale in a conversation. It was either a house going on the market or...

"Theresa!" I exclaimed. No wonder the name sounded familiar.

"You mean the crime junkie lady? She lives on this street?"

"Twenty-six Auburndale Street."

We were standing in front of eighteen Auburndale. Theresa's place was four more houses down, well before the stop sign.

"This could be the break we've been looking for," I said. "Her partner is a police consultant. If anyone has a security camera on this street, it would be him." Ignoring the remaining mailboxes, I hurried to Theresa's address.

"What if he doesn't?" Rob asked as followed me.

A crime junkie professor who specialized in the criminally insane? I would be shocked if he didn't have multiple systems. "Then we say hello, tell him what we're doing, and see if he'd be willing to help."

"A complete stranger?"

"The husband of a client," I corrected. "Who invited me to stop by for tea any time I wanted. Can you think of a better time?"

Theresa lived in an Italianate-style house that had been divided into two apartments. As we climbed the stairs to the double, frosted glass door, I spied a pair of cameras tucked in the corner of the small porch on our right. Rob saw them as well and grinned. For the first time in days, I could see a lightness in him. How I hoped their range included the sidewalk.

I rang the buzzer for Theresa's apartment. Out of the corner of my eye, I saw the curtains in the window move. In under a minute, the front door opened wide to reveal the woman of the hour.

"Sadie! How good of you to stop by!" She was dressed in a soft gray sweater and black leggings, glasses firmly in place on top of her head. She was accompanied by Benito. The little white dog greeted me with a loud bark, before looking at Rob and growling.

"Benito, stop. You're being rude. Sadie is a friend. I apologize," she said. She scooped the dog into her arms. "He tends to get upset by strangers on the street."

"Sounds like he's protective of you," I replied.

"Oh, he is. Very. Although with Christopher on the road as much as he is, the extra security is appreciated. Hello." The last part was aimed at Rob.

"Rob Carmichael. I'm a friend of Sadie's," he said. I noticed he used his posh British voice instead of his usual Northern England twang. Flashing his best smile, Rob nodded gallantly, to which Theresa gave a slight smile.

"Professor Carmichael lives down the block from your new home," I told her.

"Is that so?" She pressed a hand to her heart. "My partner, Christopher, is a professor."

"Sadie told me. I'm looking forward to having a fellow academic on the street."

Fellow academic. I had to look at my feet to keep from

rolling my eyes. I know, technically Rob was an academic, but he was…Rob.

"We walking in the neighborhood and thought we'd stop in," I said. "Is this a bad time?"

"Not at all," she said. "Ten thirty happens to be my scheduled coffee break. Why don't you come in?"

The two of us stepped over the threshold and into the building foyer. To the left, a staircase led to the second-floor apartment. To the right was Theresa's front door, partially open.

"Why don't you have a seat in the living room, and I'll make fresh coffee," she said with a smile directed at Rob. And only Rob, I should note. I hoped Christopher wasn't the jealous type.

We stepped inside.

Oh. My. God.

20

BEHIND ME, I heard Rob suck in his breath. "Holy sweet mother of God," he whispered. "It's a bloody museum."

He wasn't exaggerating. Theresa's front door entered into a combination living room/dining room area tastefully decorated in hues of soft purple and gray. The walls, however, were plastered with photographs. Large, small, color, and black & white. Some were candid shots, others were professionally taken. And they were all of the same subject: Clayvon Scott. Also known as television's Dr. Christopher Grimes from *Grimes on the Street*.

"Don't tell me this is your client's amateur detective partner?" Rob had an expression that was equal parts disbelief and dismay. After all, I'd just told him this visit could help clear his name.

"Maybe it's a coincidence. Maybe her Christopher inspired this Christopher." Even as I said it though, I knew I was grasping at straws.

I walked up to the cutout. Christopher's, that is Clayvon's, penetrating brown eyes stared back.

"I can't believe I didn't make the link," I said. An

expert in criminal behavior around whom crimes just seemed to happen? That was the entire premise of the show. I was surprised Theresa didn't mention how he was a widower still grieving the loss of his journalist wife.

"Have you ever watched the show?" Rob asked.

"Only once or twice. I'm usually asleep before it comes on."

"Then that's why you didn't make the connection. I'll give her one thing," he said as he gave the cutout the once over. "She's got good taste. If you're going to be obsessed, might as well make the obsession count, right? Did you see that she's got a copy of the swimsuit cover he did?"

"How could I not?" The poster-sized shot dominated one of the wall collages.

I shook my head. I'd seen a lot of strange things during my career, but this was among the strangest.

"What do we do now?" Rob asked.

"Have a cup of coffee," I replied. "We still need her camera footage." Film, thank goodness, wasn't delusional.

I shrugged off my coat and took a seat on her striped sofa. An expensive piece, I noted. It looked like it came from one of the upscale furniture stores. Benito joined me, standing on his hind legs, and poking his head through the crack in the curtains.

Meanwhile, Rob ambled over to examine the china cabinet. He was handling the situation well. The weirdness seemed to have given him a sense of calm.

Theresa returned, carrying a tray with a trio of mugs that were color-coordinated to match the décor. She set it on the coffee table and handed one of the mugs to me. "You'll have to excuse the mess," she said. "We rarely have visitors during the workday."

I looked around the apartment. There was a pile of papers spread across the dining room table. Otherwise, the place looked spotless. "I'm glad we caught you during your break."

"I make it a point of pausing every day at this time. Ritual is a vital tool for maintaining productivity. I see you found our collection," she said to Rob.

"Yes," he replied. "It's very…impressive. Are these all authentic?"

"Of course! I've made a point of documenting the various successes in Christopher's career. It reminds me every day how special he is and how lucky I am that we were able to connect."

The volume of collectibles in the case was astounding. I spied a pocket watch, several teacups, and what looked like an antique pipe—props from the show. There were also items from Clayvon's earlier career, like the bandana he wore in that gang war movie (which I identified only by the autographed still from the movie perched behind it).

"Are those action figures?" I asked, pointing to a trio of large-headed plastic figures.

She clutched her coffee mug to her chest. "Aren't they adorable? Christopher and I had a good chuckle over those when we saw them. Usually, he's embarrassed by attention —he's very private—but the thought that someone would commemorate his success in such a way… Well, we couldn't help being amused."

"Sounds like an interesting fellow," Rob said.

"Interesting? No, he's far more than interesting. I remember the first time I saw him. It was at the funeral for a colleague who'd died in a car accident. I could see from his eyes how deeply the death affected him. And, of course, his brilliance. The way he figured out it wasn't an accident?" She sighed and took a sip of coffee.

"The pilot episode," Rob whispered.

"That's when I knew…" Turning from us, she walked

to the cardboard cutout and brushed its cheek. "The two of us are connected by an etheric cord."

"A what?" I asked.

"She means their bond isn't an earthly one, but on a deeper level," Rob said.

"Precisely! Christopher and I communicate on the astral plane." Her face beamed with delight. "It's so nice to speak to someone who understands. I could tell you had a sensitive soul."

"Well, I do teach poetry," he said.

"Why, Christopher and I adore poetry! How marvelous. I'm so glad you found someone to fill the hole in your heart," she said to me.

"We're not together," I told her. "Rob and I are just friends."

"You're still mourning," she said.

"She's not my type. I prefer someone who looks like…" Rob gestured with his mug toward the cutout.

Theresa opened her mouth to say something in return but was cut off by Benito, who suddenly burst into loud barking.

"Not again," she groaned. "Benito, that's enough." She scooped up the little dog with one arm and moved him away from the window. The dog, however, continued to bark, his little legs paddling the air in an attempt to escape.

I peeked through the gap in the curtain in time to see a woman pushing a stroller disappear from view.

"Now you understand why we have to move," she said. "Benito gets this way every time someone walks along the street. It's impossible to concentrate."

She set the dog on the floor. Benito immediately returned to his post guarding the sofa. "Sadie told me our new street has far less traffic," she said to Rob.

"Very little," he assured her.

"Thank goodness, because both Christopher and I have had our fill of pedestrians. Especially the runners. It's as if they have zero respect for time, always out at strange hours."

Rob and I looked at one another. "What kind of strange hours?" he asked.

"Hours when normal people are sleeping. Early morning. Late night. The other night, a runner came by close to eleven o'clock! I was preparing to link with Christopher through lucid dreaming when he completely broke my trance. Took me forever to calm Benito down afterward. That was the straw that broke the camel's back. I called your office the next day."

Theresa called on Sunday. Meaning her late-night runner passed by on Saturday night. I leaned forward, trying to keep my excitement in check. My hands squeezed the coffee cup. "Are you sure it was a runner that disturbed Benito?

"Of course, I'm sure. I saw him. His headlamp practically lit up the street."

Rob and I grinned.

21

"I'm sorry you lost your sale," Rob said on the walk home.

"No, you're not." The man wasn't even trying to look sorry. He hadn't stopped grinning since we left Theresa's house.

His grin widened. "You're right. I'm not."

Needless to say, once Theresa learned that Rob was the "annoying runner with the headlamp", she wasn't thrilled to have him as a potential neighbor. "I'm moving to get away from runners," she said. She perked up, though, at the idea of being a key witness for the defense.

"Are you saying that your life is in my hands?" she asked Rob. "How thrilling. Wait until I tell Christopher."

We explained the entire situation, including our search for footage from area security cameras, like the ones she had on her front porch. Her landlord installed the doorbell camera, but as luck would have it, she was responsible for the porch cameras.

"You can never be too careful," she said as she logged into the camera's online account. Two minutes later, we were looking at street footage from Saturday night. Sure enough, at five minutes past eleven, Rob's lean figure appeared. Even with the headlamp, there was no mistaking those cheekbones.

We'd done it. Our long-shot plan actually worked. I took out my phone to call Bartlett. "I'm not sorry, either," I told him.

"You what?" Bartlett said when I told him the good news. Not the enthusiastic response I expected. "I thought you were going to trust the process?"

"I am. I do. I was giving the process a little nudge." And it had worked. We found someone to confirm Rob's story.

Bartlett promised to follow up with Theresa as soon as possible.

"He's annoyed with us, isn't he?" Rob asked when I hung up.

"Meh. Nothing we won't survive. Besides, if Theresa can get you off the hook, it's worth every bit of grumbling I get from Bartlett."

"Unless he meets Theresa and decides she's a complete nutter. Then I'm back to being screwed." He ran a hand through his blue-black hair. "I can't believe my life depends on a woman who has lucid dream dates with a fictional TV detective."

"She's obviously got a good enough grasp on reality to pay the bills." And have money left over. Those collectibles in her cabinet couldn't have been cheap. Some looked like authentic antiques.

"But does she have a good enough grasp for Bartlett to believe her?"

I certainly hoped she did. "If not, we have her surveillance tape. Film can't lie. Well, it can, but I doubt Therese is doctoring her security footage. Add in those other houses we found, and I'd say you have a pretty decent alibi, Mr. Carmichael."

"Thanks to you," he said. "I don't know how I'll ever repay you."

"Tens and twenties will do." My voice cracked on the joke. The damp sheen in Rob's eyes left a lump in my throat too big to cough away."

"I'm serious. You saved me life today." Grabbing my hand, he kissed my knuckles, glove and all. "I'm sorry I never told you about Alex and his visits," he said.

"Don't be. Everyone has a right to keep a few secrets."

A crooked smile inched onto his face, erasing the emotion from before. "That your way of saying you've been keeping things from me?"

"Hell, yeah. Tons of stuff," I said. Truth hid itself best when masquerading as a joke. "Do you think I would share my deepest, darkest secrets with a man who wears an 'obnoxious headlamp?'"

"Thank God I did. Made me that much more memorable."

"Not as memorable as Theresa." I still couldn't believe I missed the connection between her Christopher and the fictional Christopher Grimes. "Could you believe her collection?" The woman had a Christopher Grimes prayer candle, for crying out loud. "How much do you think those props and collectibles cost?"

"Depends on the demand for *Grimes on the Street* merchandise. Wouldn't surprise me if Clayvon had a rabid fanbase eager to get their hands on his collectibles. Pun intended."

"Did you ever have fans like that when you were in RU Ready?" A band aimed at teenage girls? There had to be a few stories.

"You mean crazy? No. Twitty got most of the attention." Twitty was Benjamin Twitmire, the group's lead singer. He'd gone on to a successful solo career. Rob and I once watched a movie with him in it. Every time he came on screen, Rob threw popcorn.

"More than you? You're kidding." I saw Twitty on screen; Rob with the flu was better looking.

"Anytime a girl looked at me, he told her I was gay. Did me a favor, really. Once the word got around." He shot me a sly smile. "If you know what I mean."

"I do, and I don't need details," I replied.

"I didn't plan on sharing. Some memories are best kept private."

It was nice, both seeing Rob back to his old self and hearing about Rob's band days. He seldom talked about his music career. As he put it, RU Ready was a period of his life best forgotten.

"I wonder how much our collectibles would collect online," he mused as we walked along.

I nearly stopped in my tracks. "There's RU Ready merchandise? How could that be? The band had one hit song." A lousy one at that.

"Sweetheart, we were created for merchandising. Look at me." He waved his hand about his face. "Do you honestly think I was selected for the band because I could sing? Trust me, my musical talent was a complete bonus."

"You have musical talent?"

He gave me a soft shoulder nudge. On the slick, wintery sidewalk, it was enough force to knock me off balance and nearly into a snowbank. I let out a squeal, and as soon as I regained my balance, scooped a handful of snow. My throw missed him by six inches, the snowball sailing by him and smashing on the blacktop.

"Just for that, you can forget getting an action figure for Valentine's Day," he called over his shoulder.

Whoa, wait one minute. There were RU Ready *action figures*? I could have my very own tiny lamé -clad Rob doll to put on my mantel? I was so searching eBay when I got home.

———

WE HAD TURNED onto Rob's street when we spotted a powder blue figure huddled on the curb in front of his house.

"Is that Greta?" he asked.

Hard to tell because the person was hunched over, but the blue cap and long sandy hair certainly suggested it was.

"What is she doing sitting there?" I asked. Why wasn't she at the Fitzgerald house watching the children?

She looked up with red-rimmed eyes when we pulled to the curb. That's when we spotted the oversized, fluffy cat with its head snuggled against the front of her coat.

"Eliot, what on earth?" Rob rushed to the curb. The creature lay boneless and content in Greta's arms, unruffled by his owner's distress.

"I found him sniffing under the trees," Greta pointed to a row of pine trees marking his neighbor's side yard. "I remember you saying he lived indoors, so I called to him. He came right over."

"Bad kitty," Rob cooed as he buried his fingers in the fur behind Eliot's neck. "You know you're not supposed to be outside. Damn door must have blown open again. The door latch needs replacing," he explained to me. "It doesn't always catch tightly. Eliot must have gotten curious and decided to explore. Is that what you were doing, Eliot?" The cat barely moved a muscle as Rob lifted him from Greta's arms.

"I was going to bring him to you, I swear," Greta said. "I only planned to pet him for a little while."

"Don't worry about it, Rob said. "It's fine."

"I would never hurt something that belongs to you, Mr. Carmichael."

"Greta, it's all right. I appreciate you rescuing him. Who knows what kind of trouble he'd have gotten into if you hadn't come along? Right, Eliot?"

Something about her responding smile wasn't right. Her eyes were puffy and red, as if she'd been crying. Her defensiveness about the cat was a little over the top, too. "Is everything all right?" I asked. "Did something happen?"

The au pair looked at her empty lap. "No," she said.

If I learned anything over my nearly two and a half decades of parenting, it was to never believe a child who avoided eye contact while saying no. Or anything else they say with their eyes averted, for that matter. One thing was certain: Greta wasn't sniffling over a lost cat.

"Why don't we take Eliot inside," I said. "Rob promised me a cup of tea. He'll make you one as well."

"I don't want to be a bother." Her eyes went back and forth between the two of us, obviously looking for Rob's permission.

"Don't be daft. You're not a bother. Besides, I owe you," he said.

She bit her lower lip. "Well, I am a little cold…."

"Then it's decided," I said. "We'll all go inside and get a warm drink. And maybe, after you're warmed up, you can tell us what's got you sitting by yourself on a street curb."

"All right," she said with a sniff.

Rob draped Eliot over his shoulder like a boneless, fur scarf—considering how docile a creature he was, it was astonishing he found the interest in venturing out—then held out a hand to assist Greta to her feet. As she gripped his fingers, I noticed her cheeks growing pinker. Someone had a schoolgirl crush. I wondered if Rob noticed.

Upon reaching the front door, we found the front door partially open, as Rob predicted. He kicked it shut behind us, before letting Eliot loose.

"That's right, you go think about what you've done," he said as the cat dashed upstairs. "When company's gone, you and I are going to have a long talk about house rules."

"Are you really going to talk with your cat?" Greta asked. She looked captivated by the idea.

"Of course. He needs to know he can't go running off willy-nilly whenever he feels like it. I don't care how many cat poems his namesake wrote. He still needs to follow the rules."

"His namesake?"

"T.S. Eliot. *If space and time, as sages say, are the things which cannot be, the fly that lives a single day has lived as long as we,*" he recited.

"Show off," I said. Greta, on the other hand, looked enchanted.

It took a bit of prodding from Rob, but we eventually got Greta to shed her jacket and hat and take a seat at his breakfast bar. With her wool sweater and cherubic cheeks, she looked adorable, like a living ad for hot chocolate. I immediately thought of Tim, who was currently single and could use someone cute and sweet in his life. Was nineteen too young for him?

"So where are Carter and Natalie?" I asked, once she was settled. After all, watching them was her job. "Did they have a playdate?"

"Mrs. Fitzgerald's parents took them to the aquarium

so she could rest. They said there was no need to go along."

"So, you got an afternoon off. Lucky you," Rob said.

"Are you enjoying the book?" she asked him.

For a moment, Rob looked confused until Greta reached for the copy of *Ariel* lying next to Jenn's cookies. "I'm afraid I haven't had much of a chance…"

I caught a glimpse of pink cheeks as she looked away. "That was silly of me to ask. You have so much to worry about."

"It wasn't silly at all," Rob told her. "It was very sweet of you to think of me."

His smile caused her to brighten. "My mother has the same book. She loves poetry."

"Sounds like a woman after me own heart."

"She told me my father read her poetry the night they met, and she fell in love twice. Once with words and once with him."

While they were talking poetry, Rob had set a trio of mugs on the counter before moving to the stove to heat the kettle. Out of habit, I reached into the cupboard for the tea tins from the overhead cupboard only to have Greta beat me to the punch.

"Relax," I told her. "You're the guest here. It's okay to let someone else do the work."

"Sorry. I like to be helpful."

"Nothing wrong with that," Rob said tossing her a wink from over his shoulder. Naturally, she took that as a sign of encouragement and continued setting up the mugs. Watching her place a bag of Rose Pouchong in a mug for Rob, I wondered how many people he'd trained to make his favorite drinks.

"Certainly. Mrs. Fitzgerald appreciates your help right now," I said.

"Maybe. I'm not so sure."

She was looking down again. Picking at a fingernail. Looked like we'd found the source of the problem. "What happened, Greta?" I asked."

"I was helping to organize all the food people have brought over. So much food. People are very generous."

"Yes, they are."

"When I was bringing one of the casseroles into the kitchen, I accidentally dropped it and made a terrible mess."

Ahhh. And Diane yelled. I reached across the counter to pat her hand. "Accidents happen to everyone. I'm sure Diane didn't mean to overreact. She's got a lot on her plate." What with lying about her affair and potentially being a murderer, I'm sure she was stressed.

"Oh no, not Mrs. Fitzgerald. She was resting. It was Mrs. Rothstein who yelled. She…" Her lip started to quiver. "She called me a clumsy cow, and said I was in the way."

No wonder she'd been crying. Being called a cow would cut straight to anyone's self-esteem. "This has been an emotional time for everyone," I said. "People say things they don't mean."

Greta's braids waved as she shook her head. "Mrs. Rothstein does not like me. She is angry at me because I said Mr. Carmichael didn't kill Mr. Fitzgerald." The au pair looked over at Rob, all the earnestness in the world reflected in her gaze. "You are much too kind a person to hurt anyone."

"I'm not sure I'd go that far," I said. Rob stuck out his tongue at me while Greta frowned.

"You don't think he is kind?" she asked.

"Of course, she does, luv. Sadie was joking."

Sadie needed to remember that some people were very

literal. "Absolutely," I said. "Rob wouldn't hurt a fly. In fact, we spent this morning tracking down proof of Rob's innocence.

"You did?" The au pair perked up for the first time. "What did you find?"

The kettle whistled. While Rob poured the hot water, I explained about Theresa, leaving out the crazy parts. No sense in advertising the fact Rob's alibi was on the greater-than end of eccentric.

When I finished, Greta's eyes were wider than ever. "That is wonderful news," she said, smiling. "I am so happy that you will not be blamed."

"You and me both," Rob replied. "I would not do well in prison. Check that. I would be fine, but it would take a lot of work, and I wasn't looking forward to the effort."

"Please don't tell anyone yet, though. At least not until the police have had a chance to talk to her."

"Of course. I won't say a word."

As she paused to take a sip of tea, I noticed her eyes were sparkling. The good news had improved her mood. Nothing wrong there. I was pretty sure my own eyes were smiling.

"Mrs. Rothstein said I was being disloyal, and that I was not helping anyone by saying Mr. Carmichael was innocent," she said once she set down her mug, "But I couldn't deny what I knew was true."

"I appreciate that," Rob said.

"And I'm sure once the truth comes out, Tonya—Mrs. Rothstein—will understand as well," I said.

"I hope so," Greta said. "She was so mean."

Rob patted her hand. "She was standing up for a friend, same was as you are."

"But Mrs. Fitzgerald does not—"

"Doesn't what?" I asked. She'd stopped abruptly, lifting the teacup in an attempt to silence herself. "Did something happen between Mrs. Fitzgerald and Mrs. Rothstein?"

A shadow crossed the young girl's face. "I don't know."

Oh yes, she did. It was right there in the way she stared into her tea.

Rob and I exchanged looks. "I understand," he said. "You don't feel right talking about Mrs. Fitzgerald behind her back."

"She has already been through so much," Greta said.

"Yes, she has, but if Mrs. Rothstein is doing something to upset her or make things worse, maybe we could help."

We waited while Greta contemplated Rob's comment. From the way she fiddled with her crystal bracelet and chewed, you could tell she was torn between being a good employee and wanting to get whatever it was off her chest.

Finally, she said in a soft voice. "I don't think Mrs. Fitzgerald wants Mrs. Rothstein around."

"Why do you say that?" I asked.

"I can't say for sure. It's more of a feeling."

"What do you mean?"

She chewed her lip again. "I overheard Mrs. Fitzgerald saying to her mother that she wished Mrs. Rothstein wouldn't be so… I think she said 'clingy.'"

"Interesting," I said. "I got the impression they were close." Didn't Renee say they'd moved into the neighborhood to be near Tonya and Stu?

"They were. Awfully close. I think they had a special relationship." For some reason, her cheeks turned bright red as she said it.

"No way," Rob replied. "Are you sure?"

The au pair nodded, her face growing redder.

"I saw them," she said. "Last fall. They were in the

Fitzgeralds' outdoor hot tub and didn't notice me come downstairs. They were kissing."

Tonya was Diane's lover? Tonya, who was supposedly the last person to see Alex alive? I locked eyes with Rob who responded with a set of sharply arched brows.

Looked like we had a new suspect.

22

"So, let me see if I have this right. Alex was bisexual and so was his wife?"

It was later and Greta had gone home. Rob and I had switched from tea to Jenn's cookies and a bottle of chardonnay. Following Greta's little bombshell, we did our best to pry more information out of her, but the au pair knew little beyond that one encounter. As soon as Greta realized what Diane and Tonya were up to, she hurried away before the women saw her.

"They could have been experimenting," Rob replied, munching away on a cookie. "Bottle of wine, a hot tub. Been known to happen."

"Maybe." I stared at our bottle of wine and tried to picture myself making out with either of them. "I don't think I've ever been drunk enough to make out with another woman."

"Sweetheart, you've never been drunk enough to make out with anyone. You're still in widow's black."

"That's not true."

He arched his brow.

I ignored him. Just because I hadn't acted didn't mean I hadn't thought about it. With certain people. Wasn't my fault I had *reasons*.

Actually, it was my fault.

"Regardless," I said, returning to the topic at hand, "Alex and Diane sound like a couple in serious need of better communication. Tonya and Stu, too. If you ask me, half the neighborhood could stand to attend a couples' retreat. Maybe they could get a group discount."

That's what happened when you got too friendly with your neighbors. There was something to be said about holding people at arm's length. Say what you will about me wearing widow's black, at least I didn't have to worry about someone encroaching on my personal bubble, which it sounded like the Fitzgeralds, the Rothsteins, and the Cooks did on a regular basis. "We're going to need a flow chart to keep all the interactions straight," I said.

"Gives a whole new meaning to 'love thy neighbor,' doesn't it?" Rob asked. "First, you've got Diane and Tonya snogging and maybe more in the hot tub. Then you've got Tonya coming over late at night to play chess with Alex or hook up with Diane. Who knows which?"

He frowned. "Where's Stu in all this?"

"Helping Toshelle Cook review her plans to start a catering business," a familiar honey-gravel voice asked. I blamed the wine for the tingle zipping along my spine.

Bartlett sauntered down the hall, a paper cup in his right hand. "I talked with him this morning, and he swears he and Toshelle were working on her computer until after two a.m. Your front door was open," he added to Rob by way of explaining his appearance before nodding in my direction.

"Again? The cats weren't out, were they?"

"Depends. Do you own more than the two who were

giving me death looks on the stairs?" Rob shook his head. "Then no. Did you know your latch is busted?"

"Yeah," Rob replied with a frustrated sigh. "Most of the time, it's fine as long as I remember to close it tight, but every so often I forget, and then the wind blows it open."

"Is there any chance you didn't shut it tight on Saturday?"

"Possibly. I was distracted. It was closed when I came home, I know that."

"Are you certain?" Bartlett asked.

"Positive. I remember because I left my keys behind, and I was afraid I'd locked myself out."

The lines deepened between Bartlett's eyes. "You didn't lock the door when you went out?"

"This is Woodbridge. Who locks their doors?"

"I do," I said.

"Same here," Bartlett said. "But then, I also wouldn't go running late at night."

"It's peaceful," Rob said. "You should try it."

Bartlett and I exchanged a look. I knew what he was thinking, – besides the fact Rob was slightly off his rocker. If Rob's door was unlocked and the door was wide open, then the killer could have slipped in through the front, stabbed Alex, and then disappeared the same way. Explaining why they couldn't find any footprints besides Alex's approaching the house.

The notebook was out, and Bartlett was scribbling. "You should have mentioned these details before, Carmichael," Bartlett grumbled.

"Excuse me. I had a few other things on my mind."

"Speaking of, did you talk with Theresa?" I asked.

"As a matter of fact, I did. She was excited to help."

Taking the question as an invitation to join us, he swung a leg over the stool on my left. I tried to ignore how his muscular frame filled the space, but it was difficult with his leg pressed against mine. He smelled of cold air, leather, and mint tea. A delicious combination.

"You could have mentioned she lives with a fictional detective," he said.

Rob and I looked closely at our glasses.

"I don't think she lives with him so much as the two of them have an extremely close relationship," I said.

"He's not real," Bartlett retorted. "As in doesn't exist."

"I know he doesn't exist. Did she tell you that she saw Rob on Saturday night?"

"She told me a lot of things, but yes, she confirmed seeing someone wearing orange sneakers and a headlamp running on her street around eleven. More importantly," he added, "so does her security camera."

"God bless Theresa and technology," I said. Rob and I clinked our glasses.

"You got lucky with the security footage. Otherwise, you'd still be under suspicion."

"Because Theresa's a nutter," Rob said into his glass.

"No, because you talked with Theresa. Talking to an alibi witness before calling the police? Not cool."

"We didn't know she was going to be an alibi witness."

Bartlett arched his brow. We both knew we were lucky he knew us. Rob speaking to Theresa could very well be painted as trying to influence her.

"Honestly," I told him. "The whole plan was a long shot. Finding Theresa was a bizarre stroke of luck."

"Bizarre is the perfect word, too." He smiled at me over his tea. "I'm glad you cleared Rob of suspicion, although you didn't hear that from me. Officially, I'm unbiased."

"My lips are sealed," I said, smiling back. For a minute, neither of us said anything.

"Now, will you stop and let the police do their job?"

"No worries there," Rob said. "I have no intention of doing anything that involves law enforcement for a long time."

"I didn't mean you, Carmichael. I meant her."

How quickly the rules change. Two nights ago, we were bouncing ideas off one another. I did my best imitation of a Jenn ponytail flip. "Does that mean you don't want to hear what we learned?" I asked.

A glint appeared in his green eyes. "How did I know you weren't done playing sleuth?" he drawled. His tea was resting on the counter, where he set it earlier. There was a soft pop as he peeled the plastic lid from the cup, letting the smell of peppermint float into the air between us as he leaned close. "Spill it, McIntyre."

"Tonya Rothstein and Diane Fitzgerald had a fling."

Bartlett's face didn't change expression other than the faint appearance of lines at the bridge of his nose. In Bartlett-land, that counted as a major reaction. "Says who?" he asked.

"Greta, the Fitzgeralds' au pair. She caught them getting it on in the hot tub." I couldn't resist adding a satisfied smile at the end. For someone he kept telling to butt out, I'd managed to dig up some decent information.

Rob and I waited while the mental picture played out in Bartlett's head. He picked up his tea and took a long sip. Then another. "Well, this changes a lot. Is the au pair certain about what she saw?"

"Think so," I said. "She certainly blushed like she was. I get the feeling she was a little embarrassed over catching her employer cheating on her husband."

"She also overheard Diane telling her mother that Tonya was clingy," Rob said.

Bartlett noted the information. "This au pair of yours

is a fountain of information. Interesting how she failed to share any of this with the police."

"Probably didn't think it was important," Rob said. "Everyone was focused on Alex."

"She wouldn't be the first person to remember something vital after the fact," Bartlett tapped his pen against the edge of the countertop. "But why share the information now?"

"I don't think she intended to share anything. She and Tonya had an argument. Rob and I found Greta crying on the curb and when we pressed, the information came out."

"Do you know what they argued about?"

"Me," Rob replied. "Greta defended me, Tonya got pissed and called her a fat cow."

"Clumsy cow," I corrected, "but equally hurtful."

"Bit of an overreaction for a dropped casserole," Rob retorted.

"But not for someone under a lot of stress," I said. "What's more stressful than sweating out a murder?"

Bartlett paused to take a sip of tea. "This adds a couple of new wrinkles to the case. Sounds like I'm going to have to have a little talk."

"With Tonya or Greta?" I asked.

"Both."

I tried to imagine Greta having a conversation with Dan Bartlett and came up with a picture of her looking nervous and wide-eyed. Like a chubby-cheeked deer caught in a pair of intense headlights. "Maybe I should come with you," I said.

Bartlett immediately cocked his head in my direction. "Excuse me?"

"To make her feel more comfortable. No offense, but you can be a bit intimidating."

"I'm supposed to be intimidating. I'm investigating the murder."

"I know, but you're super-intimidating."

He leaned a little closer, his eyes boring into mine. His voice dropped a notch. "How so?"

Like this. The way he locked onto a person like he was a missile. It gave the target palpitations.

"You just are," I said and grabbed my wine to wet my throat.

I had to take a second sip when the corner of his mouth ticked upward. "I'll take that as a compliment. As for your little au pair, I promise to tread lightly. I can be gentle, too."

"Good to know." Did he mean to make his voice sound that gravelly? I nearly had to bite my lip to keep my insides from getting all melty.

"Hullo? Still here."

At the sound of Rob's voice, Bartlett and I sat back and took a drink. On the other side of the counter, Rob was shooting me a probing look I did my best to ignore. I was so going to hear about this later.

"Thank you," he said. "Am I the only one who thinks it's odd that Tonya was with Alex at his house—or was supposed to be rather—while Stu was with Toshelle late on a Saturday night?"

"No," Bartlett and I said together.

"Where was Darius in all this?"

Good question. We looked at Bartlett. "Home asleep, allegedly," he said. "Same as Diane."

"Too bad they weren't sleeping together," Rob joked. "We'd have Woodbridge's very own swinger's club."

I laughed. That urban myth had been going around Woodbridge for as long as I could remember. People were always weighing in on the supposed signal to indicate a member. I've heard everything from a certain color door to a blue globe lawn ornament. There was even a rumor about candles in the window which would make the holidays confusing, if you asked me.

"Come on," Rob said. "All that cross-mingling. Don't tell me I'm the only one whose mind went there."

"Your mind is the only one that went there," I replied.

"Actually," Bartlett said, "when I worked in Baltimore, I remember hearing about multiple suburban sex clubs they busted in the Beltway."

"So, you think it's possible there's one in Woodbridge?" I knew things went on behind closed doors, but that seemed over the top, even for our town.

"All you need is a handful of couples looking to spice things up."

"Spice things up how?" Rob leaned across the granite, his eyes sparkling with curiosity.

"What do you care?" I asked. "You don't swing."

"Doesn't mean I'm not curious."

I was curious too, but I didn't need details. Not when Dan Bartlett was filling the space next to me with his oversized virility. We could Google the information later.

"Look hard enough, and you'll find a flavor for everyone soon or later," Bartlett said. "The most common are pay-to-play kinds of deals. You pay a door fee to cover party costs and then mingle as you will."

"Organized sex parties," Rob said.

I guess we were having the conversation now. I grabbed the wine and topped my glass to the rim.

"Among other things," Bartlett replied.

"That's legal?"

"It's a razor's edge, but so long as it doesn't cross the line into prostitution or blackmail or another illegal activity, then yeah. They are all over the place. Search under swingers on the Internet, and you'll get a whole list."

"That so?" Rob had his phone out and was scrolling before I could swallow my mouthful of wine.

"Did you have to get him started? Now he's going to read us all the information he finds."

"You started it by saying they were urban legends," Rob shot back. He was engrossed in his web search. "He's right, by the way. You wouldn't believe the information. Message boards. Meetups. This…" He pointed to the screen. "This is what we should be investigating, Sadie. Not chess clubs."

"You're on your own there, pal." Visiting a sex party was the last thing I wanted to do.

"I had no idea you were so straitlaced," Bartlett said.

"And you aren't?" I retorted. He was a detective, for goodness' sake.

He looked over at Rob, who was now well down the web search rabbit hole before leaning closer. His breath was warm with peppermint. "Wouldn't you like to know?" he drawled before snapping a cookie in half with his teeth.

I opened my mouth to respond, but nothing came out. I was too busy staring at his buttoned-up shirt collar and thinking inappropriate thoughts about how the Oxford cotton below stretched taut against his torso.

His chuckle came low in his chest. "Anyone ever tell you you're cute when you're flustered?"

No. At least not in a tone that made me squeeze my thighs together. "I-I'm not flustered," I said, finally finding my voice. "I'm… Why are we having this conversation?"

"Says there are often rules," Rob read from his phone. "Code words and such."

"To keep the tourists out," Bartlett replied. "These

clubs are only for people who are serious about the lifestyle."

"Check this out," Rob said. "This one site recommends using names of cities for code words, like saying 'Have you ever been to Scranton?' if you want to leave. Or drinks, like 'I would love a Screwdriver, right now.' That's not subtle at all."

"Rob, could we focus?" If I didn't stop him now, he'd be reading sex party facts all night, and I'd rather not keep discussing sex with Dan Bartlett.

"Hold on, luv," he said, holding up a finger. "You can use food terms like dessert. I would think that one would get awkward at dinner parties. They'd say, 'fancy dessert?', and you think they mean Key Lime Pie."

Or brownies...

"Sonuvabitch," I said, slapping my palm on the counter.

Rob was right.

"The word *dessert*," I explained when they stared at me. "When I was talking to Jenn the other day, she told me how she'd attended a couple of barbecues with Alex and the others, but that they stopped inviting her because she wasn't into dessert."

"And you think that when they said dessert, they really meant after-dinner activities," Bartlett said.

"Makes a lot more sense than excluding her because she wouldn't eat the marijuana brownies." Other pieces from Jenn's story fell into place as well, such as Darius giving backrubs and Diane saying Jenn didn't share the same tastes. "They must have invited her with the hopes of bringing in some fresh blood, only to dump her when it didn't work out."

"Wait a second," Rob said. "The neighborhood sex club recruited *Jenn*? What am I, chopped liver?"

"More like the wrong demographic," Bartlett replied. "Participants usually enjoy mixing it up with both sexes."

"That's discrimination," Rob said.

"Give me a break," I said. "What would you do in a

swinger's club anyway? You won't even share your popcorn at the movies."

"It would have been nice to be asked."

"I gather from your indignation then, that Alex never mentioned anything about what he and the others were up to," Bartlett said.

"Not a word," Rob replied. "Although, he did tell me that he was tired of 'the life.' I assumed he meant playing the devoted husband. Guess not."

Bartlett was writing in his notebook. "This certainly puts Diane's Sunday wardrobe in a new light. Maybe you're right, and she didn't spend the night in her own bed."

"It also explains what Greta saw in the hot tub." Diane and Tonya. Alex and Tonya. Stu and Toshelle. And now maybe Diane and Darius. I needed a flow chart to keep track of the co-mingling. "The whole thing sounds exhausting. I don't know how they do it without getting jealous. I know I couldn't."

"You and a lot of other people," Bartlett replied. "A lot of arrangements work great at the beginning, but eventually, human nature kicks in. Someone gets overly invested or decides to change the rules without letting the rest of the group know. Way I see it, there's no such thing as a free lunch."

"Could that be what happened with Alex?" I asked.

"You mean someone didn't want him leaving the group?" Rob asked.

I looked at Bartlett. "What do you think? We all think Alex came here to announce his decision to leave Diane. What if he also told someone else? Someone who we've been told is very attached to Diane?"

"Tonya."

"Exactly," I said. "She and Alex were supposed to be

'playing chess.' Instead, he pleads a headache and asks her to leave. Only where's she supposed to go? She can't go home because Stu's helping Toshelle 'go over her small business plan.' And Diane is at Darius's house doing whatever." I didn't have a euphemism for them.

"So, she decides to sit in the car until either someone's finished or it's late enough to sneak home," Bartlett said, picking up the thread.

"Except while she's waiting, she spots Alex heading here. So, she what? Realizes where he's heading and drives her car over here hoping to see what's going on?"

"Possibly," Bartlett said. "If she's in the car like we suspect. Her initial plan could have been to peep through the window. But then she finds the door open because of the broken latch."

"And Alex wandering around the house by himself," Rob piped in. "He would have looked around to see where I was."

I picked up the storyline again. "Naturally, upon seeing him, she asked why he blew her off. Alex, having decided to come clean, tells her everything. So now she's been rejected, and Alex is breaking up the sixsome. Not to mention betraying Diane. The two of them argue, it gets heated and, in a fit of rage, she grabs the knife off the counter and stabs him. She freaks out and runs out the front door."

"Leaving poor Alex to leave the kitchen and stumble through the snow, hoping to find help. Except he doesn't, and he dies alone," Rob said sadly. I reached over and squeezed his shoulder.

Having laid out the scenario, we waited while Bartlett replayed the story in his head. The wheels were turning. I could tell by the way he tapped his pen against his notebook. "It's got some holes in it," he said finally, "but it's plausible."

"More than plausible, if you ask me," I said. "Love, jealousy, and obsession. People have killed for less."

"Yes, they certainly have. Of course, all of this is based on Jenn's interpretation of events. We don't know for certain the six of them are a swingers club."

Someone was splitting hairs. I believed Jenn's interpretation. "Well, as my Jack used to say, 'if it walks like a duck and talks like a duck…'"

"It's probably a duck." Bartlett drained his tea. "I want to talk to Jenn first to get more details, but it looks like Ms. Rothstein and I are going to be having a long talk tomorrow morning."

"I've had one of those talks," Rob said. "They aren't fun."

"And you were innocent," I said. Tonya, on the other hand…

Something told me that Tonya was about to have an unbelievably bad day.

24

THE FOLLOWING MORNING, I came home and found Tim in his uniform, seated at my kitchen island, waiting for me.

"Walk of shame?" he asked, his mouth full of English muffin.

"Don't talk with your mouth full. And no, I spent the night at your Uncle Rob's. We were celebrating his getting off Woodbridge's Most Wanted List."

"I heard they found a witness to corroborate his alibi. That's awesome."

"*They* didn't find anything. Rob and I tracked her down with good old-fashioned leg work. A lesson I learned from your father."

"Dad was a good cop," he said. "The older officers still talk about him at the station. And congratulations. I'm glad Uncle Rob's off the hook."

"Thank you. So am I." Tim had made a fresh pot of coffee, bless his heart, so I poured a cup. The world was not my friend yet. After Bartlett left, Rob and I spent the evening polishing off his chardonnay collection and researching swinger's clubs. To our surprise, there were over eight hundred adults looking to swing in our area alone—or so said one of the websites. "Do the guys really talk about your dad?"

"A few of them. Kirby, Campari, McMillan. They tell me stories from when he first transferred here."

I smiled, remembering Jack in those days. I was still young and looking over my shoulder, but he'd embraced life in Woodbridge like he'd lived here all his life.

"Did they tell you the Teddy Ridgeline story?" I asked. Teddy Ridgeline had been a retired professional baseball player and local celebrity, used to getting the star treatment from the local authorities. Jack, during his first week in town, not only didn't recognize him, but took him in for multiple motor vehicle violations. For months after, he was known in town as the cop who arrested Teddy Ridgeline.

Upon my asking, Tim laughed. "Oh yeah, I've heard that one a bunch of times. There's also one about a prostitute who... Never mind. You don't want to hear it."

"I already have." Multiple times, most likely.

There was an empty carton by the toaster oven. "Did you toast the last English muffin?"

"Um, yeah," he said. "Why? Were you planning to eat it?"

"No, I just leave food on the counter in case you decide to come around while I'm out and eat it."

He gave me a sheepish grin. "Thank you, Mommy."

Damn kid. He'd played the mommy card because he knew it would melt my irritation. Plus, it was hard to claim food property rights when I also kept the cookie jar stocked with his favorite cookies.

"Never mind," I told him. "I'll have toast with my coffee. There is still bread, right? You haven't eaten that too, have you?"

"Ha, ha, ha. Very funny. I don't suppose you feel like making eggs, do you?"

I let out a sigh. "Scrambled okay?" There was some shredded cheddar on the refrigerator shelf, so I grabbed that along with half a red pepper and an onion. In for a penny, in for a pound as they say. "How's the new patrol officer working out?" I asked as I shut the fridge door. "What's-her-name? Hobbs?"

Tim groaned. "Terrible."

"Really? I thought she was supposed to be one of the academy's top recruits."

"That's what we were told."

"Then what's the problem?"

"She's just..." He frowned, looking more like Dougie than ever. "You know how some people have to act all buddy-buddy with everyone? Cracking jokes, bringing in cookies. That sort of thing."

I cracked an egg. "You're right. She sounds terrible."

"I'm serious, Mom. It's annoying. The other day, she arrested a shoplifter. You'd think she solved the Fitzgerald case, they made such a big deal about it."

"Don't they usually mark a person's first collar?"

"They do, but it's more than that. I can't explain it. She rubs me the wrong way."

Although it sounded more to me like someone didn't appreciate the newbie getting all the attention, I wasn't up for the argument the observation might cause. Therefore, I simply shrugged. "Can't always be friends with everyone you work with," I said.

Tim made a noise that sounded like a snort. "Trust me, Mom, she and I will not be friends. I'll treat her with respect because she's a fellow officer, but otherwise, I don't want anything to do with the woman."

"Speaking of women..." It wasn't the smoothest of

transitions, but it was better than continuing down the current conversational road. "You're not seeing anyone right now, are you?"

"Thank you for the reminder. Why do you ask?" He shot me a look before picking up his coffee.

"Because there's this girl…"

"Ma…"

"Relax. I'm not trying to fix you up." Well, I was, but only in the most casual of ways. "She's the Fitzgerald kids' au pair. Greta. She's from Germany, and I don't think she knows too many people her own age. The only people she sees are the other families in the neighborhood. I thought, maybe, once the murder was solved, you could…"

He washed down the piece of muffin he was chewing. "You *are* trying to fix me up."

"I'm not. All I was going to do was suggest you introduce her to your friends. Help her get to know people younger than your Uncle Rob."

"Let me guess, she's got a crush on him."

I thought of the adoring way she looked at him every time Rob spoke. "A little one," I said, "but that's beside the point. She's a sweet kid who could use some friends."

"When you say kid, what do you mean? How old is she?"

Good question. It was hard to tell. "Around twenty," I said. Given her naiveté, she could be younger than that. "Or nineteen."

"I doubt my friends are going to want to hang out with someone that young."

"Because you all are so old."

"I'm going to be twenty-six soon," he replied.

Dammit, he was. Meal sponging aside, he'd gone and grown up on me. In my head, he was still a teenager. Sometimes I forgot how much time had passed. When I was his age, I'd already betrayed my family and gotten pregnant with him.

"And then there's the trouble I'd get into if an underage girl was caught with alcohol while hanging with us," he said.

"Point made. I just hate seeing her pining over Rob is all. She looks at him like he's some kind of rock star. And I don't mean in the lame-ass way he was a rock star. I mean like he makes the sun rise and set."

His six-foot-two frame joined me at the counter. "I wouldn't stress too much," he said, handing me an egg. "Eventually, she'll figure out she's not Rob's type and move on like everyone else."

"You're probably right." I cracked the shell against the edge of the bowl, wondering for the umpteenth time in my life how cooks on television did it with one hand. I always had to pry the two halves apart and then pluck pieces of shell out of the egg white.

Tim handed me another egg. "How is Uncle Rob doing, anyway?"

"Today? Probably moving slower than me, but I think he's relieved."

"Word at the station is that the woman who cleared him is a bit loony."

I reached for a knife to chop the pepper. "I thought there was a rule about saying things about witnesses behind their backs."

"I'm only repeating what Dan Bartlett said."

"Is that so?" Bartlett seemed like the last person to disparage a witness. "Did he call her loony?"

"He said she was quirky, whatever that means."

It meant Bartlett was the gentleman I suspected he was. "She is a little different," I said, "but her security footage is one hundred percent reliable.

"The more I think about it," I continued, "I'm not sure Theresa is as much different as she is lonely." Why else would a woman befriend a fictional character other than she desperately wanted friends?

"Maybe you should introduce her to your au pair friend. They can be each other's new friend."

If I didn't think Theresa would terrify Greta, I would. "Don't worry about Greta," I told him. "I'll find someone else to chat her up, since you're not interested."

"Ah-hah!" he shouted. "I knew it was a fix-up."

"It was not. I simply..." I gave up. Why bother fighting a lost battle? "Okay, fine. I might have been hoping you two hit it off."

"I knew it. You're a terrible liar."

If only he knew. His entire life had been built on a lie. A damn huge one.

Over the past six months, I'd been thinking more and more about that lie, too. For some reason, what had once seemed solid and secure had begun to feel shaky. I don't know if it was Marylou's murder proving that my identity wasn't as hidden as I thought, or Tim's growing resemblance to his birth father, but the knowledge that I was keeping the truth from people I loved weighed heavier than ever.

Shaking off the thought, I grabbed my whisk and started beating the eggs, switching the conversation back to the murder as I stirred. "You've never answered any disturbance calls or anything in Rob's neighborhood, have you?"

"You mean like domestic disturbances?"

"I mean reports of anything unusual. Calls about loud parties, arguments..." Backyard orgies getting out of control...

He shook his head. "The call log was one of the first

things Bartlett asked about. Only call was for a dog running loose in someone's backyard. Why?"

"I was curious, is all. Now that your Uncle Rob is no longer considered a suspect, I figured attention would be turning to other people in the neighborhood."

My phone rang before Tim could respond. "Probably Keith Koenig. Renee posted a new listing yesterday. No doubt he wants first dibs on rejecting it. I better take the call. He's been skittish since the last property had a dead body."

But the caller wasn't Keith. It was Rob, and he was out of breath. "You're not going to believe this," he said. "While I was out for my run, the police blocked off Poplar Street."

"A police barricade? Why?" I looked over at Tim, who mouthed "Where?"

"Not sure," Rob said, "but there's an ambulance parked in the Rothstein's driveway. Saw it when I cut through the backyards to see what was going on. And Sadie?" He paused. "They were wheeling out a body."

25

TIM AND I DROVE TOGETHER. Or, more precisely, Tim insisted on driving me. To keep me from getting in the way, he claimed. Really, though, he was as curious as I was about what happened.

Poplar Street ran parallel to Evergreen, where Rob lived. Like Rob's street, it boasted mega-sized colonials with professionally landscaped yards. It was where the Cooks, the Rothsteins, and the Fitzgeralds all lived. And, for the second time in four days, home to a dead body.

Therefore, we weren't surprised to see the orange roadblock signs sitting in the center of the street, with a squad car parked not far away. Further, down the block, a collection of blue lights lit up the cloudy morning. Tim parked the car at the top of Evergreen, and we headed to Poplar Street on foot.

When we got there, we saw two officers sitting in the car. One was George Vasquez—I'd recognize his bald head anywhere. The other a petite blonde with her hair pulled tight in a bun. They both gave us a look as we rounded the corner.

Beside me, Tim groaned. "Hobbs," he muttered when I glanced at him.

Vasquez lowered the window. "What gives, McIntyre? They call you in too?" That was when I remembered Tim still had on his uniform.

"Nah, I was checking in on my mom when she got a phone call. She's got a lot of friends on the street. I told her I'd bring her over so she could make sure they were all right." From behind his shoulder, I waved hello.

There was a small crowd gathered two houses down. I spotted Rob's orange sneakers among them. Leaving Tim to talk with Vasquez, I walked to join him. He stood with Jenn and Greta on the sidewalk in front of the Fitzgerald house.

As usual, Jenn looked like an Instagram photo for a wellness resort—compression leggings, a coordinating designer ski jacket, and a matching wool headband. I was beginning to think she woke up perfect-looking. For a man who drank himself silly the night before, Rob looked disgustingly good, too. Only Greta, in her jeans and puffy ski jacket, looked like a normal person. She stood with her bare hands folded together as if in prayer.

Rob greeted me with a kiss on the cheek. "Morning, luv. Can you believe all this?"

The activity centered on the Rothstein house. A pair of officers were examining the shoveled walkway while another searched around the front stairs. A fourth officer stood at the end of the driveway to keep curiosity seekers like us at bay. I noticed Bartlett's dark SUV parked in the driveway.

"They took the body away five minutes ago," Jenn said.

"Who was it?" I asked. "Do you know?"

"Tonya, I think, but no one will say for sure."

I looked at Rob, both of us thinking the same thing.

Just last night, Tonya Rothstein became the top name on Bartlett's person of interest list.

"Any idea what happened?" I asked.

"No clue," Rob said. "None of the police officers would talk to us."

Maybe they'd be more open to one of their own. Tim was heading toward us. I gave him an entreating smile.

"No," he replied.

Wow. He sounded more like Bartlett than either of his fathers. "You don't know what I'm going to ask."

"Yes, I do. You want me to get details on what happened."

All right, he did know. "Will you?" I asked.

"Mom! This is an active crime scene."

"I'm not asking for a detailed forensics report. We just want to know if the victim was Stu or Tonya."

He did his best to look aggravated at my request. Problem was, I could tell that he wanted to know the details as badly as we did. "Fine," he said after a minute. "I'll see what I can find out." The snow crunched beneath his shoes as he stepped off the curb and headed across the street.

"Now, hopefully, we'll find out for certain. What makes you think it was Tonya?" I asked Jenn. If it was her, it was an improbable coincidence that she would die so soon after we uncovered her affair with Diane.

"When they were removing the body, I thought I heard someone say to be 'careful with her'. But they could have said 'it.' I'm not sure. Either way, it's awful."

One thing was certain, the sixsome would never be the same. My attention slid one house over to where the Cooks stood on their front step, Darius's large hands on Toshelle's shoulders. She had a winter coat over her bathrobe and was dabbing at her eyes.

"I saw the cops talking with their daughter," Rob said. "I wonder if she's the person who found the body."

Oh man, I'd forgotten about their kids. They had a son away in college and a daughter finishing her senior year of high school. They and the Fitzgerald children were innocent victims in all of this.

"I don't understand why all these terrible things are happening. First Mr. Fitzgerald and now this. It's so terrible." Greta's glassy eyes threatened to boil over, and she began blinking rapidly. "It's so frightening." Rob put his arm around her, and she burrowed close, sniffling into his shoulder.

"Two people dead on the same street within days. What are the chances?" Jenn asked.

"Pretty rare," I replied. This death had to be connected to Alex's. It was way too coincidental not to be.

"Poor Mrs. Fitzgerald," Greta said, her head still resting on Rob's shoulder. The beads on her bracelet caught the sunlight as she wiped at her tears. "She's lost so many people. First her husband, now her friend."

"She's going to need you more than ever to help around the house," Rob said.

A gleam of determination appeared in Greta's eyes, inspired either by Rob's words or the little side hug he gave her. She pulled herself a little taller and sniffed away her tears. "I will not let you down," she said.

"More importantly, don't let Diane down." The way that girl looked at Rob... Someone was going to have to speak with her. Rob, too. He should know his little fatherly routine was causing a case of hero worship.

I returned to watching the Rothstein house. Tim was in the driveway talking to one of the officers in the driveway. A broad-shouldered woman I didn't recognize. After a few minutes, he clapped her on the shoulder and headed to us, a grim expression on his face.

"Did you find out who it was?" I asked him.

He nodded. "The deceased is Tonya Rothstein—"

At the mention of Tonya's name, Jenn gasped. "I can't believe it."

Neither could I. "Did they say how?"

"Head injury. The cleaning crew found her lying on the kitchen floor when they arrived this morning."

"When you say head injury, what do you mean? Did she fall or…"

"They're still investigating."

"Still investigating" said to me that this wasn't an accident. That meant someone wanted Tonya dead. Probably the same person who killed Alex. From where I stood, there was only one person in the sixsome with strong enough connections to both victims.

Diane.

26

"OFFICER MCINTYRE!"

Dan Bartlett's sharp voice cut across the neighborhood, causing all of us to stand at attention. He strode toward us like the man in command that he was. And while he may have called Tim's name, his focus was on me. I could feel the heat of his stare from across the street. His gaze remained on me when he reached us. You'd think by now I would have learned not to wilt under the scrutiny, but no such luck.

"I didn't realize this was Bring Your Mother to Work Day," he said, his precise enunciation voice making it clear he wasn't making a joke.

"Sorry, Detective. She was going to come anyway. I figured it was better if I came too, so she couldn't cause trouble."

"I'm not sure that's possible. Trouble seems to follow her."

"You don't have to address me in the third person. I'm standing right here." Also, my son was totally throwing me under the bus. The liar wanted to come as much as I did.

Bartlett finally acknowledged me. "I suppose you've already nosed around and discovered what happened to Tonya."

"I know that someone killed her," I replied, adding, "You wouldn't be hanging around if she died accidentally."

He arched his brow, but nothing more. "I see the gang's all here. Rob. Jenn. And…" His blue eyes locked on Greta, who quickly broke away from Rob. I mentally apologized for suggesting he'd frighten her.

"This is Greta, the Fitzgeralds' au pair."

"Pleasure to meet you, Greta." His tone was a one-eighty turn from the way he addressed Tim. Like he was approaching a kitten. "Did you see anything unusual this morning?"

The au pair shook her head. "No, sir. I wasn't aware of anything until Mrs. Fitzgerald pointed out the police cars. I told her I would find out what had happened. It is all so sad. Poor Mrs. Rothstein, dying over her morning tea." Her eyes began tearing again. She blinked them aside. "Mrs. Fitzgerald is going to be so upset. Mrs. Rothstein and she are—were—very close."

"How close?" Bartlett asked.

"I don't understand the question," Greta replied. Apprehension flickered across her face. I thought I knew why. She was worried about telling tales out of turn. Gossiping with Rob and me was quite different from sharing information from the police.

I watched as Bartlett schooled his features into a gentle expression to match his voice. "You said the two were very close. Were they best friends? Like sisters?"

"Maybe? Why does it matter?"

"Because it's possible Mrs. Rothstein's death wasn't an accident," Bartlett told her. I was afraid the news would cause the girl to break into tears again, but she held herself together. A few unshed tears, but that was it.

"Are you saying that she was murdered like Mr. Fitzgerald?" Immediately, she looked at Rob with fear on her face. Worried he was in trouble again.

"You don't have to worry about Rob," I said. "He's not a suspect. I can vouch for his whereabouts. We were together until around seven this morning," I told Bartlett, who took notes.

"There's a surprise," Jenn said. "It's only your second home."

"See? Rob is no longer in trouble." I gave Jenn a side-eye. "But that means Mrs. Rothstein's killer is still out there. You have to tell Detective Bartlett everything you know, even if that makes things awkward for Mrs. Fitzgerald."

Rob slipped around her again and gave her shoulder a squeeze. That seemed to do the trick more than my pep talk. "All right," she said and told Bartlett about the hot tub.

Bartlett nodded as if it were the first time he'd heard the information. "In the times you saw them together, did you ever see them argue?"

"No. Not with each other. Although…" She glanced at Rob, who gave her an encouraging smile. "Mrs. Fitzgerald did speak very abruptly to her yesterday afternoon."

"What do you mean?" Bartlett asked.

The au pair fiddled with her bracelet. You could tell she was trying hard not to make her employer sound bad. "Mrs. Rothstein has been spending a lot of time at the house, helping Mrs. Fitzgerald. Yesterday, she told Mrs. Rothstein to go home."

"Do you know why?"

"No, but she was angry to hear Mr. Carmichael would

no longer be a suspect. I told them the news when I got home from your house yesterday afternoon," she said to Rob. "She and Mrs. Rothstein both said the police were idiots to ignore all the evidence."

Bartlett's smile momentarily tightened, but he quickly recovered. "I appreciate your candor. For what it's worth, I'm glad Mr. Carmichael is no longer a suspect as well."

"That makes three of us," Rob said.

"Five," I corrected, making sure I included Jenn in my count. After all, the woman was standing with us.

"Let's just say a lot of people are glad and leave at that, shall we?" Bartlett said. "Must have been difficult believing in Mr. Carmichael's innocence when your employer thought otherwise. You're a good friend"

The au pair gave a tiny smile. "*Danke.*"

"*Bist du Deutscher?*"

"*Ja. Hamburg.*"

"*Eine meiner Lieblingsstädte. Es ist sehr schön dort.*"

I'm not going to lie. The fact that he seamlessly slipped into German was hot.

Greta offered a timid smile. "*Danke.*"

"Must be hard for you, living in a small town like Woodbridge, away from your friends and family."

"A little, but the people here have been so nice to me. Mr. Fitzgerald. Mrs. McIntyre. Mr. Carmichael."

Bartlett was busy scribbling in his notebook. "I noticed you didn't mention Mrs. Fitzgerald. Do you get along with her?"

"I…" She worked her jaw up and down, kind of like a fish gasping for air. "Yes, we get along. She's different than Mr. Fitzgerald. That's all."

"Different how?"

"She's…scarier? I don't know if that's the right word."

Bartlett smiled a slow smile, a warm, honeyed smile I

was surprised didn't set the snowbanks to melting. "Maybe if you tell me what she does that's different, I can figure out the better word."

Cheeks getting a little pinker, Greta lowered her lashes. "She is very particular in how things need to be done. And when they aren't, she gets upset."

"Does she lose her temper? Yell?"

"Only once. She was upset that I let Carter have chocolate pudding before bed, and she slapped the counter so hard it made the dishes rattle."

"Imagine if you did that whenever I snuck a snack before bed…" Tim whispered in my ear. "The counter would have a hand-shaped dent."

So, Diane had a temper. If she'd slap a counter over pudding, what would she do if she learned her husband was planning to leave?

Bartlett was making notes. "You must have to wake up early. If I remember, three-year-olds don't like to sleep in. At least my girls didn't. How about the Fitzgerald kids?"

"Natalie is a late sleeper. Carter, he is up with the sun."

"You were up and about this morning, then. Did you see anything unusual? People roaming about or strange cars?"

She shook her head. "I was in the kitchen getting Carter a cup of cereal. I couldn't see the street. May I go now?" she asked, as she glanced over her shoulder toward the Fitzgerald house. "I told Mrs. Fitzgerald I would not take long."

"Of course. I appreciate the information." Bartlett began to tuck the notebook in his jacket when he suddenly appeared to think of something, stopping Greta before she could leave. "One more question, if it's okay. Do you happen to know what Mrs. Fitzgerald did last night?"

"Mrs. Fitzgerald? She went to bed early. She said she was tired."

"Was that the last time you saw her until this morning?"

"Yes." She cast another nervous glance at the Fitzgerald house. "May I leave now?"

"Of course. Thank you for the information. You were very helpful."

The group of us watched her hurry up the driveway. "Interesting tidbit about Diane having a temper," I said.

"Lots of things are interesting," he replied with his usual lack of expression. "Makes me wonder what else the au pair has seen around the neighborhood."

"Makes me want to watch what I do in front of the hired help," Jenn said. "If I ever get hired help."

We all made a similar mental note.

Having finished his interview with Greta, Bartlett made a point of walking us to the corner before returning to the crime scene. I should have complained about the unnecessary show of authority. Problem was, he was holding my elbow ever so gently the entire way. Whenever he touched me like that, the contact wiggled its way to my insides to distract me. How could a man stand in the cold and yet radiate so much body heat?

"McIntyre, I'll talk to you at the station," he said when we reached the corner. Without looking, I could see Tim cringing.

"Yes, detective," he replied.

"And could the rest of you do me a favor and go about your business? I've got enough on my plate without worrying about spectators damaging my crime scene."

"You don't have to ask me twice," Jenn said. "I'm freezing. Besides, I told Erin I'd meet her at Cuppas. She's already ticked that I blew off yoga. You two want to join us?" She turned her big blue eyes to Rob. "We've missed seeing your pretty face the past three days. The place is not the same."

"Appreciate the offer, luv," Rob said, "but I don't think I'm ready to leave my hermitage. Especially considering…" He nodded backward, indicating the Rothstein house. "People might talk."

"All right, if you're sure. I'll catch you later. By the way," she added as she leaned in to kiss his cheek. "Those people can stuff it."

You know, Jenn might annoy me with her perfect hair, her perfect clothes, and her perfect face, but I couldn't say she wasn't the perfect friend. What with her forgiving me for suspecting her of murder last fall, and her unwavering loyalty to Rob, I was going to have to adjust my attitude toward her. Damn, but I hate self-growth sometimes.

Bartlett turned his attention to us. "How about you two?"

"I'm with Jenn. It's bloody freezing," said Rob. "I'm going home and taking a long hot shower. I've had more than enough excitement this week, thank you very much."

"And you, Mrs. McIntyre?" He had a look that said he wanted to pin me in place. "Are you going home to shower as well?"

"If you are asking if I plan to do something stupid, the answer is no, I do not."

"Good. Like I said, I have enough on my plate without worrying. About civilians." I wondered if anyone else noticed the beat between sentences. Or how we held each other's gaze two or three seconds longer than necessary before Bartlett tipped an imaginary hat and walked away.

Someone had. "What the heck was that?" Tim asked.

"Nothing to worry about. Just your mother and Detective Bartlett dancing around the obvious," Rob replied.

"Now if you excuse me, I have a date with a shower and a large cup of coffee."

"Me, too. The coffee part, anyway," Jenn said. "Talk to you later, Sadie."

My mind was already back on Poplar Street as I watched them walk away. All I could think of was that less than a week ago there were six neighbors tightly entwined in each other's lives. Now there were four. To continue Jenn's animal metaphor, had Diane decided to cull the pack of weak links? There was only one couple left unscathed. If something had been going on between Tonya and Diane, chances are Darius and Toshelle knew. And, considering the nature of the goings on, as well as their potential involvement in them, the two of them might be more comfortable speaking to a neighbor than to the police.

Looked like it was time to pay another condolence call. But first…

"Coming, Mom?" Tim asked.

First, I had to ditch my kid.

27

DITCHING Tim wasn't an easy matter as I *had* promised to make him an egg breakfast and he tended to eat a lot. It was two hours and six eggs later when I pulled into Rob's driveway.

"We need to talk to the Cooks," I said when he answered the door.

He leaned a shoulder against the doorframe, his arms folded across his cashmere sweater, keeping me on his front step. "Funny, but I could have sworn Bartlett told us to mind our own business. How does talking with Darius and Toshelle fit into that plan?"

"They are the only couple left intact. If anyone knows the skinny on what was happening with Tonya, Stu, Alex, and Diane, it's them."

"You didn't answer my question. How is talking with them minding our own business?"

"Short answer?" I said. "It isn't." The long answer involved a gleam I caught in Bartlett's eye suggesting he didn't expect me to follow his request and was, in fact, hoping I wouldn't since neighbors talked to neighbors far more easily.

Rob would tell me that was a lot to read into one blue-eyed sparkle. That's why I gave him the short version.

"At least you're honest. Let me get my coat."

Three minutes later, the two of us were on Rob's back deck. "You got new mittens," I noted as I zipped my coat. In place of his driving gloves, he wore a pair of arctic knit wool mittens that on anyone else would look childish, but on Rob qualified as quirky.

"Told you, the bloody things were useless. Found the missing mate behind the bench in the boot room. Now I'll be able to feel my fingers."

Darius and Toshelle's backyard was situated diagonally from Rob's house with the Rothsteins living on their right. Stu and Tonya's yard was adjacent to the house on Evergreen that I'd been showing. It was on that property line where Alex took his final breath.

Poplar Street remained blocked, and police cars were still in the Rothsteins' driveway which made knocking on the Cooks' front door impossible. The next best solution was to cut through a gap in Rob's neighbor's forsythia and make our way to the patio doors. As we went by the snowman, Rob stopped to replace the red knit hat the wind had blown off and straightened one of his arms.

"Creepy, I know," he said, as he adjusted one of the sculpture's blue mittens, "but I feel like I should maintain it seeing how it's the last thing Alex touched. Even if it was to stab the thing."

"Not creepy," I said. "Sweet."

"Thanks." He brushed his mitten across the rust-colored stain still visible after four days. "He looked a lot jauntier with his scarf, but it must have blown off."

"You'll find it in the bushes this spring." Many lost items were found once the snow melted.

"Whatever. Won't be wearing it again anyway," he said, a feeling I completely understood as the scarf would be forever tied to Alex's last moments.

It was hard to look at the sculpture and not think about how only hours before Alex jammed a knife into the snowman's side, his children had been building it. What had been going through his mind? Had he realized he would never see his children again?

"What exactly are you hoping the Cooks will say?" Rob's question broke the melancholic atmosphere.

"Something that might confirm Diane was having an affair with Tonya. Or that she didn't spend the night with Darius."

"So, we're back to Diane being the killer."

From where I stood, which was ankle-deep in snow, she seemed the most obvious choice. "Even if Tonya killed Alex, Diane could have found out and lost her temper. They could have fought and—"

"Somehow Tonya bangs her head."

"Or Diane bangs Tonya's head for her."

"Funny." Rob held aside a forsythia branch to make an opening in the bushes. "Diane never struck me as the hotheaded type. I always pictured her more like a shark. You know, the kind who would hunt her prey slowly and deliberately."

So did I, to be honest. Even sharks had a breaking point, though. Maybe Tonya found it.

We crossed into the Cook's yard. I could see Darius's broad back in his large, pass-through kitchen window. From the movement, he looked to be drinking coffee. Hopefully, he and Toshelle were alone and not, say, entertaining Dan Bartlett. Stepping up onto the patio, I stomped the excess snow from my feet and knocked on the glass door.

"Hey," Rob greeted when Darius answered.

Sometimes I forgot how large Darius was until I was standing close, craning my neck to look him in the eye. He looked stressed with thick, black stubble on his face and bags under his eyes. "What are you doing at my back-door?" he asked, looking at Rob. "Why didn't you cross the street when you were here earlier?"

I jumped in. "We would have, but Detective Bartlett asked us to leave, so we cut through Rob's yard. We wanted to tell you how sorry we are about Tonya."

"Sucks," was his short reply. He continued to look at Rob. "Heard you're off the hook for what happened to Alex. They found a witness or something." News traveled fast.

"Something is a good word for it," Rob replied. "Would it be okay if we came in? It's a bit nippy out here."

Darius looked uncertain.

"We won't stay long," I said.

"All right." His long breath looked like a tiny plume of smoke in the cold. "But take your shoes off at the door so you don't trek the snow in the house."

"Sounds like Toshelle's got you well-trained," I joked.

"Oh, it's not Toshelle's rule; it's mine. I don't like a dirty house. Dirt's a gateway to germs, you know."

And sharing spouses wasn't? My eyes sought out Rob, but he was too busy toeing off his wet running shoes to look at me. I stepped through the door, slipped off my ankle boots, felt my socks to make sure they were dry—wet socks no doubt were as off-limits as wet shoes—and looked around.

I'd never been inside the Cook's house. I suspected,

based on Toshelle's and Darius's stylish appearances, that the house would be gorgeous as well, but I was unprepared for how calm and tranquil the décor was. The light wood was complemented by soft shades of turquoise and brown. It was like stepping into an upscale spa but with much better furniture. I remember Toshelle once joking that she banished all of Darius's memorabilia to his man cave downstairs. I could see why. Football trophies would totally kill the vibe.

We'd entered the breakfast nook. Based on the half-eaten avocado toast on the table, they'd heard the news during breakfast.

"I was just cleaning up," Darius said as he scooped up the plate.

We followed him into the kitchen, which was decorated in the same soothing browns and blues. "We wanted to see how you were doing," I said. "I know Stuart and Tonya are good friends."

"Great friends. I can't believe…" He ran a hand over his closely shorn curls. "First Alex, now this? Diane said someone hit Tonya on the head. Why would someone do that to her?"

"I'm sure the police will find out," I said.

"Hope so. We all thought for sure we knew who killed Alex and look how that turned out. No offense," he added for Rob's sake.

"None taken," Rob replied.

The two of us leaned against their quartz countertop and watched as Darius washed the dirty dishes. His movements were slow and dull, far from the world-class athletic moves he was famous for. Now that I thought about it, his voice was the same way. "There's coffee if you want some." Without waiting for an answer, he took a pair of mugs from the cupboard and poured. "I keep thinking it's a mistake. That Tonya's fine and it was someone else they brought outside."

"I know the shock," I said. "My husband, Jack, died almost a decade ago. Took months before I stopped thinking I could hear his footsteps in the foyer."

"What did Tonya ever do to anyone? Everyone loved her."

He handed us each a mug of black coffee. I looked around for cream and sugar, but there didn't seem to be any. Darius didn't seem to be offering any, either. "All I can think of is that some druggies looking for cash must be breaking into houses and Tonya scared him. What else could it be, right?" he asked, his brown eyes silently urging us to agree. "They probably broke into your house and Tonya's."

A random, third party breaking into houses and killing two people from the same street? Darius had to know he was reaching. Or was he trying to deflect suspicion from someone? Like Diane.

"Did you see anyone?" I asked.

"Not really. Some kid in a hoodie maybe? Then again, maybe not."

"What do you mean, maybe not?"

"Duval has been his usual sixth-grade self and dragging his feet about getting up for school. I was busy trying to get his sorry butt out of bed so I'm not sure what time I looked out the window. Maybe if I'd paid more attention…"

"You might have gotten hurt, too," I said.

He scoffed. "Toshelle said the same thing, but I could have handled a doped-up kid. I could have distracted him or scared him off or something."

Call me naïve, but he sounded sincere to me.

"Stu turned around as soon as he got word. He's going

to go straight to the high school to get Tiffany. He told the school he wanted to be the one… Oh." There was the soft rustle of silk as Toshelle came floating into the room wearing a kimono-style robe and leggings. Her braids hung loosely around her shoulders. She stopped and stared at Rob.

"Innocent," Rob said. "No longer a suspect. Came by to express condolences."

"So, I heard. Good for you." Flowing by us, she stood with her back to the kitchen while she poured a cup of coffee.

"We heard you say you talked with Stu," I said once she'd turned around.

"Yeah. Poor guy left before dawn so he could drive to New York for a meeting. He was feeling guilty about going —he thought he should stick around here once we realized the killer was still on the loose—but Tonya told him he was being silly."

Her lower lip started to tremble. Moving around us once more, she made it to the kitchen counter. There she stood with her arms straight out, her hands gripping the counter edge. I could see her shoulder muscles rippling beneath the silk. "It doesn't feel real," she said in a shaky voice. "I feel like I'm watching one of those movies where the stupid teenagers get chased through the woods by an escaped lunatic. Only, we're not in a movie. Alex and Tonya are really dead. And the lunatic is still out there." Her head dropped as her shoulders began to shake.

Darius joined her. Standing to her side, he rubbed gentle circles between her shoulder blades. Speaking to her in a gentle voice, he said, "Everything will be all right, babe. I promise."

"Can you?" I caught a glimpse of the worry etched on

her face as she talked to him from over her shoulder "I bet Stu made Tonya the same promise."

She shook off his touch. "I'm sorry," she said, to no one in particular. "The stress of everything has got me feeling a little paranoid."

"Perfectly natural, seeing as how you've lost two friends," Rob said. "You're scared that what happened to Alex and Tonya might happen to you or Darius."

"Exactly." She gazed into her untouched coffee. "I feel we're being targeted. Silly, right? Why would someone target us?"

"I don't know," I said. "You tell me."

Toshelle looked at me when I spoke. It was clear from the challenge in her eyes that she knew that I knew *something*. "What are you getting at?"

Somewhere, there was a list of the top ten most awkward questions to ask your neighbor. I used to think "Did you know our kids are having sex" and "Did you kill your neighbor" were the top two, but "Do you and the neighbors swing?" beat them both. I'd already asked people the first two questions. By asking today, I would be completing the trifecta of awkwardness.

"Word around the neighborhood is that you two, the Fitzgeralds, and the Rothsteins are very close."

"Very, very close," Rob repeated with emphasis.

The nostrils flared on Darius's flat nose. He stared at me with narrowed eyes. "So?" he asked.

Dancing around the subject was getting us nowhere. I decided it was time to be direct.

"So," I said, looking him in the eye, "I hear you're a big fan of dessert. And I don't mean edible munchies."

28

Toshelle and Darius looked at one another. You could almost hear their silent conversation. Subtle, they were not. "Where did you—"

"Toshelle." Darius tried to cut her off only to receive a glare, the silent message quite clear.

"Don't Toshelle me, Darius," she said. "Two of our friends are dead. What difference does it make at this point who knows about us?"

"But Diane—"

"Diane can go pound sand."

Darius spun around to the sink in defeat. "Fine." Grabbing the sponge, he began wiping out the sink. "Go ahead. People will probably find out anyway."

I saved Toshelle from answering. "It's true then. The six of you were swingers?"

Despite her grief-stricken state, Toshelle managed a derisive sniff. "The way you say it makes us sound like we wear gold chains and play Barry White all night."

"What do you do, then?" Rob asked.

She blinked. "Have sex. What else would we do?"

"Look, I love Toshelle. She's my soul mate," Darius said. "But that doesn't mean I don't like a little variety now and again."

"Having the same meal every night can get boring, even if it's filet mignon. The way Darius and I see it, why not sample the buffet? Makes the beef taste that much better."

With her hands cradling her coffee cup, Toshelle flowed toward the dining room with her head high. I got the feeling this was a speech she and Darius had given before. "When Darius and I first got together, we wasted way too much energy fighting over stupid jealous stuff. This groupie came on to him; this guy took my phone number. Eventually, we realized that we could either fight about these other people, or we could work together to make sure we're mutually satisfied."

"It's the ultimate team sport," Darius said. "Being with someone and knowing my Toshelle's being satisfied at the same time? Makes the sex that much sweeter."

Toshelle blew him a kiss. "Now the only thing we argue about is keeping the bathroom clean."

"Damn body washes and makeup all over the place," Darius muttered.

"How did the Fitzgeralds and the Rothsteins get involved?" I asked.

"That was a stroke of luck," Toshelle said. "The six of us met at a swingers' party a few years ago. We've been enjoying one another ever since."

"Like a group relationship," Rob said to her.

"Not like you're thinking."

"But you all moved into the same neighborhood," I said.

"For convenience," she replied. "You don't have to

worry about arranging for sitters or worry about what time you're going to get home. But we still go out, too."

"Convenient can get boring too. For the past year or so, we've been trying to recruit other people to add some variety, but vetting takes time. Not everyone's a good fit," Darius said.

"You mean like Jenn?" I asked.

Toshelle rolled her eyes. "Poor Jenn. So beautiful, and so slow on the pickup. She actually thought we were talking about dessert."

"Still does," Rob replied.

"Now you know our story." Darius leveled his dark brown eyes at Rob and me. There was an expectancy behind his stare. "Is this the part where you decide we're a bunch of sexed-crazed degenerates?."

"Not me," I said. "What you do is your own business." Like I was in a position to judge anyone for their behavior.

"Well, that would put you in the minority." Darius came up from behind and wrapped his arms around her waist. She rested her head against his chest. "In the end, it doesn't matter what people think. The arrangement works for us. Or it did. Until…"

Darius pressed a kiss to the top of her head.

"Is that lack of understanding the reason you told Greta you had a neighborhood chess team?" I asked.

"That was Tonya's idea. I told her it was a weak excuse —no one plays chess all night—but she went with it anyway."

"That was Tonya for you," Darius said. "Once she got an idea in her head, nothing could change her mind. And some of her ideas were good ones."

"Suh as the six of us moving to the same neighborhood," Darius said. "Diane wasn't sure she wanted to move, but Tonya was determined to convince her, remember? All those barbecues where she'd go on and on about the school system?"

"She was right," Toshelle said. "Woodbridge does have good schools."

"Renee Drake said Tonya was the one who found a house for Diane."

"She did. She was dying for them to be closer," Toshelle replied. "It made sense. Diane and Alex wouldn't have to worry about driving home. We could take our time enjoying the night. Plus, Tonya and Diane were best friends. What could be better?"

"And no one ever developed feelings for someone other than their spouse?"

"Of course, we developed feelings. We all care deeply about each other," Darius said. "It's what makes the arrangement work so well."

I thought about what Diane said, about Tonya being clingy. "What if someone decided they felt more deeply than the rest of you?"

He frowned at me. "What are you trying to say?"

"Was it possible Tonya developed deeper feelings for Diane? Maybe even fell in love with her?"

"No way," Toshelle said, shaking her head. "No way. Diane wouldn't allow it. She was strict about maintaining the ground rules."

"What about Tonya? How did she feel about the ground rules?"

"She was a loving woman." Darius released Toshelle from his embrace and folded his massive arms across his chest. His eyes glowered. "Why are you asking all this about her, anyway? The poor woman is dead."

"I know," I said. "I'm merely looking for answers, and Tonya..." Darius's eyes narrowed, and I gulped some air before continuing. "Tonya was the last person to see Alex alive."

Toshelle took a step forward; I raised my hands. "You are the ones who said she was stubborn, and we've heard that she was extremely attached to Diane."

"They were best friends. Are you suggesting that she... what? Killed Alex because she wanted Diane to herself? No way. Tonya wouldn't hurt a fly." She spat the words with defensive anger.

They were loyal to the group, I'd give them that.

"Even good people get consumed by jealousy," I said. "Or grow overprotective, if they think someone they love is going to get hurt."

Darius's face wrinkled in confusion. "Get hurt how? We all had each other's backs."

"Not everyone's," I said. "We think Alex was planning to leave."

"No, he wasn't."

"Yeah, he was." Rob's soft voice caused the room to go silent. "That's why he was at my house that night. We'd been talking for weeks. He told me he was tired of the lifestyle. At the time I didn't realize what he meant, but now I do."

Toshelle and Darius looked shocked. "I don't believe it," Darius said. "We were tight. If he was having problems with the lifestyle, why would he talk to you and not one of us?"

"Probably because he didn't want you to know he'd leave her for me."

For the next several seconds, the only sound you could hear was the ticking of the kitchen clock. There wasn't even noise on the street outside.

The look of betrayal on Toshelle's face said it all. "You and Alex were having an affair?"

"No. I don't sleep with married men, swingers or otherwise. But something was growing between us. The night of the murder, he told me he had something important to tell me. I think it was that he planned to leave Diane."

"Which was why he blew off Tonya that night." Darius was slowly putting the pieces together.

"Exactly," I said. "And if Tonya thought Alex was going to divorce Diane and possibly embarrass her with a local scandal, she might have lost her temper."

Darius shook his head. "No."

"He's right," Toshelle said. "I don't know if Tonya had feelings for Diane or not, but there's no way she killed Alex. Absolutely zero percent chance. And I can prove it."

Following her proclamation, Toshelle folded her arms. She cocked her head and waited for me to ask.

Naturally, I did. "How?"

She flashed me a satisfied smile. "Because when Alex begged off, Tonya joined Stu and me," she said. "The three of us were together the whole night. And Tonya slept in the middle."

29

WE RETURNED to Rob's the way we came, having accomplished little. If anything, the water surrounding Alex's murder was muddier than ever. Toshelle swore that Tonya and Stu were with her all night. Darius copped to being with Diane, but he also swore the woman never left his bed. "She was in a hungry mood," he told us. "We didn't stop until dawn."

"Five people and five alibis," I said. As well as five mental pictures I wished I didn't have.

"Clearly, someone is lying," Rob said.

"Valuable deduction, Sherlock." I shivered, not from the snow, but from the icy goodbye we got from the Cooks. Guess I could forget about seeing them at any more of Rob's barbecues.

With Tonya's whereabouts verified, we were back to square one, leaving me puzzled and cranky. "Two people are dead. You'd think they'd be motivated to talk for their own safety, if not to preserve their neighborhood reputation."

"Unless they're afraid to talk," he offered. "Two dead

neighbors are also a motivation to stay quiet. Who wants to cross a psycho?"

Two dead people and an innocent man nearly arrested, I thought. They'd better be good and scared.

Yellow police tape waved from the branches of the forsythia branches, as though Alex's ghost was contributing to the conversation. If only he could.

It was time to rethink the situation. "Let's look at the group logically," I said. "We can rule out Stuart. He was driving to New York when Tonya was killed." And, even if he wasn't, Toshelle swore they were together all night.

I bent over so I could scoot under a branch. "Toshelle's out too. I can't think of a single reason she wanted either Alex or Tonya dead. Darius, maybe—he was the one sleeping with Diane."

"Unless she and Darius decided they would eliminate one another's competition."

"You mean like *Strangers on a Train* but with spouses?" I pondered the suggestion for a moment before shaking my head. Tonya and Diane. Darius and Diane. Toshelle and Stu and Tonya. All the different combinations were making me dizzy. It was like a murder puzzle cube where you had to keep turning the sides until you found the one combination that clicked the others into place. Instinct told me the solution was far more straightforward than we were making it.

I stopped to stare at the snowman, whose arm had fallen off again. What were we missing? The answer was right there staring us in the face, I could feel it. The question was, could we solve the puzzle before someone else ended up dead?

30

As BADLY AS I wanted to sort out the questions in my head, I was taking a client around to view properties at four this afternoon. With all the craziness of the past three days, I'd been shirking my Realtor responsibilities.

It had been a slow winter, business-wise. I didn't want to tell Rob, but Theresa withdrawing her offer on the Wiggins property hurt. I tried to salvage the sale by promising that Rob was the *only* runner on their end of the street, but she and "Christopher" were afraid Benito would be traumatized by his running. She asked me to find something else.

Adding insult to injury, Keith Koenig emailed to say he and his wife needed to take a break from house shopping because of Sunday's "trauma."

Lucky for me, my clients, the Travinos, were motivated buyers. I showed them six properties. They fell in love with house number three, a delightful Federal with an above-ground pool, going so far as to make me drive by the house a second time. I made a point of emphasizing the open house being held over the weekend—delightful houses always sold at open houses—and by the time we said good-bye, I was ninety-nine percent certain they would be calling with a proper offer.

Nothing lifts my spirit like the prospect of a commission. To celebrate, I decided to treat myself to takeout from the Golden Panda.

Woodbridge had two Chinese restaurants. There was the Koi Garden where you went for Mai Tais and gourmet Hunan specialties. And then there was the Golden Panda. Located in Woodbridge House of Pizza's old spot at the strip mall, the Golden Panda featured the finest in deep-fried goodness from column A and column B. If you were jonesing for an egg roll and fried rice or chicken lo mein, the Panda was your place.

No sooner did I step through the restaurant when Mrs. Travino texted with a couple of questions about the property taxes and water bill. They were definitely making an offer. I started texting back while making my way to the counter, only to collide with a wall of muscle and leather. The delicious scents of peppermint, bath wash, and sesame oil filled my nostrils.

The wall turned, revealing Dan Bartlett's scowling face. When he saw me, the scowl morphed into a lazy smile. "Don't tell me we're going to have to make texting and walking a ticketable offense," he remarked, his gaze dropping to the phone in my hand.

I tried to shake off the excited sensation that erupted when I saw him. "Shouldn't you be at a crime scene?" I asked.

"Shouldn't you be bothering me at a crime scene?"

Did he know how comments like that made my stomach flutter? "I'm celebrating the impending sale of a house," I told him.

"Congratulations. I take it no one stumbled over a dead body there."

"Not this time. For once, I had the serendipitous pairing of an easy-to-please client and the perfect property."

"Good. I'm glad." His voice softened with sincerity. The feeling washed over me like a verbal massage. Fluttering eased into a feeling of comfortable camaraderie.

"Can I buy you dinner?" I asked, my potential windfall making me magnanimous. "I owe you for the pot roast. Or are you heading back to the station?"

"Actually, I came here to be alone and run some theories through my head. But," he added quickly, "since you're here, I wouldn't mind bouncing them off you."

I forgot all about my plans for takeout.

We placed our orders and helped ourselves to one of the red laminated booths that lined the wall. A backlit photograph of the Imperial Palace, the electrical cord drooping, marked our place. Far less romantic a surrounding than Gilroy's, but as Bartlett slid across from me and unzipped his jacket, I had to remind myself that while this was the second time we'd shared a meal, it was not a date. We were two people with a mutual interest in a murder.

"Congratulations again on the sale," he said. "Is this the house Rob's alibi wanted or a different customer?"

"Different one. Theresa decided to pass on the Wiggins property," I said as I peeled the paper from my chopsticks. I don't know why I bothered unwrapping them. I was only going to swap them out for a plastic fork before the meal ended. "One too many joggers for her dog's liking."

"Wow. Her dog must really hate joggers if she's willing to pass up a house that had a dead body in the backyard."

"I know, right? Houses with amenities like that don't

come on the market very often." At least I hoped they didn't. "Although technically Alex's body wasn't in the Wiggins's backyard. He was in the Rothsteins'."

"I know. Two inches over the property line." He pulled out the insides of his eggroll. Unlike me, the man handled his chopsticks like a pro. "Two inches over, and two hundred yards short."

"Excuse me?"

"One of the things I've been running through my head," he said. "Alex died only a few hundred yards from his front door."

He'd almost made it home. Made you wonder if he would have survived had he finished the journey, or if someone had found him sooner.

Bartlett seemed to read my mind. "Not sure making it all the way would have made a difference. According to the ME, his fate was sealed the minute the knife plunged into his chest. Removing the knife only hastened the inevitable. Doubt the poor bastard was thinking about that, though."

I pictured the knife stuck in the snowman. "It's like he wanted us to find the knife. Makes you wonder what he was thinking. Beyond, 'Oh my God, I've been stabbed.'"

"Bringing us to the second thought floating through my head," he said. "Several of Alex's actions don't make sense. There were houses all around. Why didn't he bang on someone's door? Instead, he walks past the next-door neighbor, past the Cooks' house, and collapses in the Rothsteins' backyard."

Especially since he knew his friends were home and awake. "It was dark," I said. "He might have been in shock. Could he have gotten disoriented and started walking without knowing where he was heading? Or…"

While I was speaking, I'd been attempting to pull my eggroll's innards apart like Bartlett had, only my chopsticks were refusing to hold on to the cabbage. They kept slipping from my fingers and clicking together. I gave up and picked up the eggroll with my fingers. "Maybe all he wanted to do was get home."

"Doesn't seem logical, but I don't how logical many people are when they're bleeding out. I've found dead bodies in some pretty weird circumstances. Half the time, we never figured out why."

"Jack, thank God, didn't find too many bodies," I said. "Unless they were at accident scenes or people who died of natural causes. It's what he liked about being a small-town cop. He was done with random street violence."

"I didn't realize Woodbridge wasn't his first beat."

"He was a cop in the city before we met." I purposely left the location vague so he would assume Boston. "We came here because we thought it would be a town where nothing ever happened."

We both smiled, remembering Bartlett's comment from Sunday night. "Glad one of us got what they asked for," he said.

"I'm sorry you haven't so far." I meant it.

Jack used to say there were a lot of ways the job could hurt you, beyond physical injury. The things they saw, the things they ignored for the greater good—they left a mark. Bartlett had the eyes of a man who looked like he carried a lot of marks. "The bodies in weird places," I said. "Were they the reason you wanted a place with no action?"

"Partially. Partially, I wanted a fresh start." He frowned into his tea. "I'd made a mess of things in Baltimore."

"I'm sorry."

"What do you have to be sorry for? You aren't responsible."

Maybe not, but I felt bad anyway. Dan Bartlett didn't strike me as a man who made mistakes easily, nor took them lightly when he did. "Well, if it makes you feel better, you're not alone. I've made a few messes myself."

"Of that, I have no doubt," he said. "From what I can see, you have quite the spirit for adventure."

Something about the way he smiled made my cheeks hot. "It's a relatively new habit, I assure you," I said.

"If you say so. How was your visit with the Cooks, by the way?"

My lo mein fell from my chopsticks. "You know about that?"

Instead of answering, Bartlett left the booth. He returned with a plastic fork. "I suspected that's what you were planning when I left you on the street corner," he said, handing me the utensil. "The Cooks confirmed it when I spoke with them."

I knew I'd seen a sparkle in his eye. "So you know that Rob was right about the swinger's club," I said.

"And that all five of them have an alibi for the night of the murder? I do," Bartlett replied.

There was a note of doubt in his voice. "You don't believe them?"

"Well, if they are as close to one another as they claim, who's to say they aren't lying to protect one of their own?"

Bartlett had a point. However, I had trouble imagining Toshelle and Darius lying. Like I said before, maybe I was being naïve, but I think Darius believed the murders were random—or at least he had until I suggested otherwise. On the other hand, I knew better than anyone the lies people would tell to keep loved ones safe.

"Could you do it?" I asked him.

He gave me one of his looks, one brow arched higher than the other. "What? Lie to protect my own?"

"Be part of a group like that." I meant what I said to Toshelle, about not being in a position to judge, but not judging an arrangement and understanding it were two different things. "Call me old fashioned, but I wouldn't have been so easygoing about sharing Jack with other women."

Bartlett's eyes had grown shuttered as he pushed the fried rice around his plate. *Terrific, Sadie. You touched a nerve.*

"Forget I said anything. It's none of my business," I said.

"My wife had an affair," he said in a low voice.

Ouch. I wasn't surprised, though. Cops and extramarital affairs went together like peanut butter and jelly: They were commonplace. "Occupational hazard," I said. The term slipped out.

"So I've been told." He pierced a steamed dumpling with the end of his chopstick. "Wasn't really her fault. I was a workaholic. She was lonely. And my best friend was extremely accommodating when it came to providing her with a shoulder to cry on. How could she resist?"

"I'm sorry," I said. It was a lame response. Then again, what could a person say to alleviate the sharp pain of betrayal?

"Better to stab me in the heart than in the back. It'd hurt less," my father had screamed when I testified against him in court. I wondered if Bartlett thought the same way. Probably.

On the other side of the table, Bartlett was stabbing the dumpling a second time. "Took me a year to realize what was going on, too. When I first had suspicions, they lied straight to my face and told me I was imagining things. Took me six more months before I stopped believing them."

"I'm so sorry." It was my turn to reach across a table and touch his hand. He looked at me in surprise when I did. "I can't imagine how betrayed you must have felt."

"The lying hurt the most," he said. "The lying and the gaslighting. If they had been honest with me from the start... She told me the reason they lied was because they didn't want to upset me. So instead, they made me feel like an irrational, jealous idiot for six months. How is that better?"

The chopstick pierced the dumpling one final time, the force of penetration sending moisture erupting from the hole. "I will forgive a lot of things in this world," he said, "but lying isn't one of them."

"Never?"

"Relationships are built on trust, Sadie. You can't trust a liar."

Something inside me sank. I'd let myself forget about my lies for a few moments. Bartlett's story was a reminder that I'd burned my chance six months ago.

"You're right," I said and hoped my disappointment didn't show.

The atmosphere had grown heavy. Bartlett had the look of a man who'd shared more than he intended. He looked at his plate, suddenly invested in the food there.

"So now what do you do?" I asked. "Regarding the investigation?"

My question pulled him from his reverie. He looked up, his mouth a tight line. "Return to square one and look at everything a second and third time. I feel like the evidence is right there, staring everyone in the face, and we're simply not seeing it."

It was an echo of my thoughts from the morning, only voiced with more frustration. "I was so certain the killer was Tonya," I said. "All the puzzle pieces fit. Or they did until she was murdered."

"Conveniently so, too. Tonya and her lawyer had

agreed to come by the station this morning to discuss what she knew about Alex's death."

Only someone killed her before she could. Bartlett was right, the murder was an extremely well-timed coincidence. "Are you thinking someone killed Tonya to stop her from talking to you?"

"The thought crossed my mind."

I sat back and watched Bartlett finish his tea. There was only one person I could think of who had reason to silence Tonya. The same person who had reason to see Alex dead.

We'd gone full circle and landed on the same person I suspected from the start: Diane Fitzgerald.

31

The following afternoon, I stood in Rob's house once again, staring into the yard. The snowman looked gray in the dimming light. Darkness still came early, but not as early as the month before. It reminded me that this whole business started as a party to celebrate the approaching spring.

Despite the cold, the snowman seemed to realize his days were numbered. His other arm had fallen to the ground, leaving him limbless. He sat there, with nothing but a crooked red cap on his head and a fading stain on his midsection.

What had you been thinking, Alex?

"Still can't find my baseball jersey anywhere."

I turned around to see Rob carrying a large cardboard box into the dining room. Two similar boxes were already lined up on the dining table. "I've looked everywhere. The closets, the laundry. Even called Tim. He said he bought his own."

He set the box next to its mates, wiped his hands on his

jeans, and then ambled over to where I was standing. "You looked a million miles away."

"Watching the snowman," I told him. What I was really doing was trying to picture the final minutes of Alex's life. Imagining him stumbling from the patio into the snow, pulling the knife out of his chest and… I couldn't get over the stabbing of the snowman. Most people would have simply let the weapon fall to the ground. Alex took the time—and effort—to plunge the knife into the snow. That suggested it was deliberate.

Why? What kind of message was Alex trying to send?

I sighed. "It's driving me crazy."

"What is?"

"The snowman. Not knowing why Alex stabbed it."

It was his turn to sigh. "There's a lot we'll never know. I keep replaying our argument Saturday night. If I'd only bothered to hear him out or stayed home instead of going out for that stupid run. Maybe he'd still be alive. Tonya, too, for that matter."

"You didn't know, Rob. You couldn't have known."

"So I keep telling myself. Doesn't make me feel better." He joined me at the patio door where we both watched the snowman turn darker with shadow. "Poor guy keeps losing his arms."

"He is limb-challenged," I agreed. "Want me to go outside and fix them?"

"Nah. The wind will only blow them loose again. I'm thinking I might put him out of his misery tomorrow."

"You mean knock him down? I thought you wanted to keep him around for as long as possible, as a sort of memorial?"

"I was, but then Greta said looking at him made her sad, and I started thinking maybe he makes the others in the neighborhood sad, too. Last thing I want to do is upset Carter and Natalie."

"Can the kids even see it from their house?"

"Beats me, but Greta's got a point. Keeping him around is rather morbid."

I'd found his reverence to be rather sweet, but seeing as how it wasn't my backyard, I kept my mouth shut.

Suddenly, something he said clicked with me. "When did you see Greta?" I asked.

"This afternoon. She came by to retrieve her mittens. That's how we got to talking about the snowman in the first place. She's a sweet kid."

"Be careful there," I said. "You don't want to get in trouble."

He waved me off. "You forget, I've been teaching kids her age for a long time. She's looking for a father figure. We spent the entire visit talking about her mother. Did you know her mother saw RU Ready live when we played in Germany? Not many people can say that."

"Literally," I added, earning myself a shove.

"I'll have you know we had a small, but loyal following in Europe, Germany especially. Will you stop staring at that snowman?"

"I'm sorry! I can't help myself." The damn thing had become a fixation. A frozen, misshapen puzzle piece I couldn't make fit and I couldn't figure out why. Just like the murders, I felt like the solution to what bothered me was *right there*, and I couldn't see it.

"Why did Alex stab the snowman?" The question sounded like one of those children's riddles. *Why did the chicken cross the road? Why did Alex stab the snowman?*

"If I didn't have an answer to your question five minutes ago, I'm sure as hell not going to have one now," Rob replied.

"How about five minutes from now?" Maybe if I asked enough times, the answer would pop out at me.

The sky was dark gray at this point. My view of the backyard had become obstructed by my reflection in the glass. Not quite ready to give up, I reached over and flipped the light switch. Mr. Snowman appeared once again, bathed in white light. For a moment, I thought I saw one of the shadows in the rear of the yard move and I tensed, until a rabbit sprinted across the snow.

"I told Bartlett it's as if Alex stabbed the snowman so that someone—you—would see it," I said to Rob.

He turned and looked at me with a frown. "When did you see Bartlett?"

"Last night at dinner."

"Oh, really? The two of you have had a couple of dinner dates lately."

"They weren't dates." I said. "The two of us just happened to be eating while we talked."

"Sounds like a date to me."

"*About the murders.*" I didn't need Rob building my relationship with Bartlett into something it wasn't. Namely a relationship. "And we're getting off topic. Bartlett and I were talking about the knife and wondered why Alex chose to stab the snowman instead of simply letting the knife fall to the ground."

"He had a knife in his chest," Rob said. "I doubt he was thinking clearly."

"Exactly what Bartlett said, but what if Alex *was* thinking? What if he stabbed the snowman on purpose?"

"To leave me a message."

"Well, it is your yard," I said.

"Wasn't a very clear message then, if that's the case, because I haven't a clue." Letting out a very final-sounding breath, he turned away from the glass. "Maybe we'll get lucky, and Diane's alibi has crumbled, putting us out of our misery," he said.

Wouldn't that be nice? I wasn't getting my hopes up, though. If Diane had confessed, we would have heard, if not from Bartlett then from the grapevine. Thus far, we'd had radio silence.

Wondering if a different angle would give me a fresh perspective, I tilted my head sideways. It didn't. What were we missing?

"Did you take any pictures during the party?" I asked Rob.

"A few. Mostly I was busy cooking. Why?"

I wasn't sure. But, staring at the snow sculpture in the present wasn't working for me. I might as well see what I could spot in the past. "Can I see them?"

"Have at it." He tossed me his phone.

Turned out, Rob took more than a few, a lot of them selfies of Rob with various neighbors. Rob with Jenn. Rob with Jim Chu. Another one of Jenn, this time waving a red foam finger. There was one of Bartlett and me chatting by the buffet. I texted that one to my phone. I continued swiping, looking for one that had a good view of the snowman. The best I could find was a photo of Darius manning the grill with the snowman waving its red hands in the background.

Something about the shot wasn't right.

I was in the process of zooming in when the sound of scissors sliding through packing tape being pulled loose caused me to look up. Rob was opening one of the boxes he'd set on the table.

"What are doing?" I asked. I'd meant to ask him when the first box appeared, but the snowman distracted me.

"Remember when I said we had merchandise? Seeing Theresa's collection of Grimes collectibles got me wondering how much some of the RU Ready stuff might fetch online. God, I haven't looked at some of this stuff for nearly twenty years."

Pulling the tape off the box, he opened it and pulled out a mile-long, red and gold silk scarf. He draped the cloth around his neck. "What do you think?"

"I think you look like you're attending wizard school."

"That's what I was afraid of." He continued rummaging through the box.

"Is my Rob doll in there?" I asked.

"Action figure, thank you very much, but you're going to have to wait till Valentine's Day. Here, you can have one of these instead," he said, holding up a bag of beaded bracelets. "RU Ready jewelry. Wear your devotion on your arm. I was sky blue. To match me eyes." He tossed me one. "Here. Now everyone will know I'm your favorite."

I put on the bracelet. It wrapped around my wrist twice, like one of those mantra bands. Whoever handled RU Ready's marketing knew what he was doing. The beads caught the light in a way that did resemble Rob's eyes. I could see young boy band fans wearing them and swooning over the resemblance. Their own little piece of Rob…

I frowned. "I've seen this bracelet before," I said, "Or something like it."

"Not surprised. You can buy something similar at every arts and crafts store in the country."

"Maybe, but I don't think so. You said each member had their own color. Do you remember what they were?"

"I think so. I was royal blue, Chico was green, Trent was this goldish color, and Twitty was this weird pale gray-ish-blue."

"Like the color of water," I said.

"Exactly. The rest of us loved how he got the ugliest color. Why?"

I didn't answer. It had to be a coincidence. The bracelet wasn't even the right color! Still, seeing it prompted me to look at the snowman again. I unlocked Rob's camera and looked at the picture on the screen. Darius's body took up most of the frame. I zoomed in on the space behind his left shoulder to get a closer look at the snowman. It looked just as I remembered. Baseball hat, red scarf, red mittens.

Except yesterday, the mittens Rob adjusted were blue. Meaning someone had replaced them after the party.

"Greta came by to retrieve her mittens," Rob had said. Greta, who helped build the snowman. The one person whose alibi no one questioned.

"I was right. Alex was leaving a message," I said.

"What are you talking about?"

"The snowman. He was trying to tell us who stabbed him. The person who built the snowman." The answer had been in our faces all along.

"But Greta and the children were the ones who built him. They couldn't…" Rob's eyes grew wide. "You think Greta killed Alex? That's absurd."

"Is it? Look." I showed him the photograph. "You didn't lose your mittens. She switched them."

Rob started at the image. "It doesn't make sense. Why would she switch her mittens with mine?"

"I don't know. Maybe to have something of yours? I bet your red scarf didn't blow away, either. There's your missing shirt, too."

"Now you're being ridiculous. No one took my shirt. I probably left it at the dry cleaners. Besides, what possible motive would Greta have to kill Alex? He was her friend.

He was helping her get into an American university, for crying out loud."

"He was also competition."

"Wha-? No way. She's just a kid."

"We think of her as a kid," I said. "She's nineteen years old and is massively infatuated with you."

He shook off the comment along with everything else I'd said. He unwound the scarf from around his neck and tossed it on the table. "Your friend Theresa is starting to rub off on you. This isn't a Lifetime movie, Sadie. There isn't a psycho nanny living across the street obsessed with keeping me to herself. If she were, wouldn't you have been the first target?"

One would think that. On the other hand, crimes can only occur where there's opportunity. I've never been alone with her long enough for anything to happen.

"Don't forget..." Rob was still arguing his point. "Greta's helped us with this investigation. We wouldn't have known about the swingers' club if she hadn't told us about Diane and Tonya. Nor about Diane's temper."

"As well as the fact Diane was having an affair," I conceded. Now that I thought about it, we wouldn't know a lot of things if it weren't for Greta's revelations. Our little au pair was useful to know.

"Every piece of information she fed us directed the investigation toward the Poplar Street sixsome," I realized. "She's been feeding us breadcrumbs."

Rob was having trouble buying the idea, I could tell from his expression. He still thought Greta was a sweet girl who belonged on a cocoa tin. Part of me did, too, but the pieces were lining up. "There are too many connections to ignore," I said. "Greta made the snowman. Greta's mittens were on the snowman. Greta provided us with key clues. Greta suggested you knock down the snowman which would make it harder to remember details like the color of switched mittens."

"All right, I get your point." He walked over to the patio door and stared outside, studying the yard. "She helped clean the kitchen after the police left. Bleached the floors and walls. I thought she was being nice. More likely, she was washing away any forgotten evidence, huh?"

"Maybe a little of both. She does like you, after all."

"What about Tonya, though? Where does she fit in? Even if Greta did kill Alex, what reason did she have to kill Tonya?"

"Tonya could have discovered something about Alex's murder or said something that upset her. I don't know."

Rob turned away from the window. "I'd feel better about your theory if you did."

"So, would I," I told him. Tonya's murder was the one question I couldn't answer. There was one person who had all the answers, though.

It was time for another talk with our favorite au pair.

32

FOR THE FIRST time in the history of our acquaintance, Diane Fitzgerald looked terrible. Oh, her outfit—black jeans, rose cashmere hoodie—was as stunning as ever, but her hair was flat and there were black smudges around her eyes.

She was also drunk as a skunk.

"What the hell do you want?" Her attempted snarl came out slurred. She compensated by taking a slug from the amber liquid in her tumbler. "Are you here to question me, too? Afraid the police didn't do a good enough job?"

Before I could answer, she walked off, leaving me in the open doorway. I followed, finding her in her white living room. An empty bottle of whiskey sat on the coffee table.

"I'd offer you a drink," she said, "but there isn't enough for two."

"Actually, I wanted to speak with-"

"It was awful, you know. Talking to the police. They asked questions about my marriage, about Tonya, about my sex life—like who I sleep with is any of their friggin' business. Judgmental little pricks. I could see it in their eyes. Just like you."

She waved her glass at me, sloshing the golden contents against the rim. "Darius told me about your little visit this morning."

Clearly, I wasn't getting out of the room without some conversation. I looked around for some sign that Greta might be listening in, like last time, but the swinging door remained firmly closed. "No one's judging anyone," I said. "We're just trying to get to the truth about who killed your husband and best friend."

"Then maybe you should focus on harassing real suspects instead of bothering me. I am a well-respected member of the bar! Alex was the father of my children. Most likely. Even if he was leaving me for Carmichael's cute little… All of him. I'd never hurt my husband."

"I believe you," I said.

"You do?" She drained the glass in one swallow. Then stared at the empty glass in shock. At its emptiness or my support, I didn't know. "I need another drink."

"I also know you wouldn't hurt Tonya," I said, as I followed her into the kitchen.

"I wouldn't," Diane said. She began rummaging through a cupboard pulling out various bottles of liquor until she found one she liked. All the while she continued talking. "I loved Tonya. She was a pain in the freaking ass, but I loved her. She was a wonderful person."

While she rambled, I looked around for Greta. The au pair had to be somewhere close by. I didn't want to tip my hand by looking too eager.

Diane, meanwhile, wasn't going to let me leave. "I knew Alex would leave eventually. He always said I was enough of a man that I didn't need to be married to one. You know what I said?"

"I don't—"

The doorbell rang. "Oh, for Chrissake, who is it now?" She glared at me as if I knew. "Coming!" she called.

This was my moment to slip out gracefully. "While you're answering, I'll head up to-"

"What is it with people tonight? I said I'm coming!" Diane screeched when the doorbell rang a second time. She jabbed a finger at me. "Stay here, I'll be right back."

Like I was going to listen to her. As soon as the door swung behind her, I headed across the room to the rear staircase. Greta was probably up in her room.

In the other room, I could hear Diane talking agitatedly. Something about Alex and harassment. A moment later, a familiar, gravel-laced voice spoke over her.

"I'm not here to speak with you, Ms. Fitzgerald," Dan Bartlett said. "I'm here to speak with Greta Strobl."

"You too? Why is everyone so interested in her all of a sudden?" Drunk Diane was not as quick to make the association as Sober Diane would be.

"We have questions to ask her, that's all. Is she home?" The kitchen door swung open and Bartlett strode into the room. He took one look at me standing at the foot of the stairs and crossed his arms.

I waved.

Diane raised her glass. For a moment I thought her eyes might roll back in her head. "She's upstairs in her room. Probably still sobbing like a drama queen because I 'ruined' her life."

"What do you mean, ruined?" I asked.

"Ruined. Like in destroyed. Smashed to smithereens. I told her I was selling the house and moving in with my parents, and she acted like I killed someone."

Bartlett and I cringed simultaneously. Diane took another drink. "She'll get over it," she said. She had the glass in her mouth as she spoke, making them muffled. "I told her I'd write her a decent referral."

This wasn't good. If I was right about Greta, that she killed Alex because he was competition for Rob's affection, then there was a good chance the au pair would see Diane's announcement as another attempt to separate them.

"Greta's room is this way," I told Bartlett and pointed to the stairs.

"May I ask what you're doing here?" Bartlett asked as we climbed to the second floor. Diane stayed behind, preferring to refill her whiskey.

"Same thing you're doing," I said. "I wanted to talk to Greta. I take it Rob told you my theory about the snowman."

"I didn't talk to Rob."

Meaning something else made him look at Greta. Quickly I explained about the mittens being swapped out and my theory as to why Alex left the knife.

"You're sure the mittens were hers?" he asked.

"Rob said she came by to retrieve them today. Why are you here?"

"Something she said on the sidewalk this morning. I didn't catch it until I ran through my notes, but she said that Mrs. Rothstein died over her morning tea. I'd never said anything about the crime scene. How would she know that Tonya had a cup of tea steeping on the kitchen counter?"

She wouldn't. Unless she'd been the house.

We reached Greta's bedroom. Bartlett stood behind me, then whispered in my ear. "You do the talking. She'll be more inclined to open the door if she thinks it's you."

"Greta? It's Mrs. McIntyre. May I come in?"

No answer. Bartlett reached for the doorknob and opened the door.

Greta was nowhere to be seen. The only indication she'd been in the room was an indentation on her pink gingham pillow sham.

"Damn," Bartlett muttered. "She must have slipped out while Diane was in the living room." He started looking around, searching the tops of her bureaus and opening her closet door.

I bent down to check under her bed. It was Tim's favorite hiding place as a kid.

Nothing.

As I grabbed the bed for support standing up, I saw a white nylon cloth sticking out from beneath the checkered ruffles. I pulled it free.

It was a Boston baseball jersey. Number 34.

My pulse went into double time. "Dan?" I called. "I found something I think you need to see."

"So did I."

I turned to see him standing in front of Greta's closet wearing the grimmest expression I'd ever seen him wear. Considering he usually looked grim at work, my heart raced faster.

"What is it?" I asked.

"See for yourself."

I looked inside. At the rear of the closet, there was a small wicker basket filled with items. A red scarf and a pair of red mittens lay on top. But that wasn't the scary part.

On the wall, was an old publicity picture of RU Ready. In it, Rob, Twitty, Chico, and Trent wearing their trademark lamé caps, posed for the camera. Someone had drawn a circle around Rob's head. Above it, they'd written the word VATER.

I looked over my shoulder at Bartlett who knew what I was about to ask.

"*Vater* is German for father," he said.

33

I was out the door and down the stairs in a flash. I heard Bartlett calling for a squad car as he hurried along behind me. I wasn't going to wait for anyone. Rob needed to know about Greta now.

Greta thought Rob was her father? Impossible. But even as I thought that, my mind pulled together the clues I'd missed. The story she told about her father reading poetry and how her mother attended the RU Ready concerts in Germany. She'd been dropping hints the entire time and we missed it.

I left my car in the street and cut through the Rothstein's backyard. It was the route. Yellow police tape passed in a blur. When I reached the property line, I saw Rob standing with his back to the sliding glass door. He was talking to someone and holding them at arm's length.

Greta.

She must have slipped out of Diane's house and come straight to Rob's. The shadow I saw earlier in the yard wasn't a rabbit. It was Greta, watching Rob's house, and waiting for the best time to approach.

I jumped onto his deck and banged on the glass. They both started.

"Sadie! What a surprise! I wasn't expecting you back tonight." His smile was stretched unnaturally wide and tight. Anxiety twitched in his eyes. "Look who else came by."

He stepped aside so I could better see Greta. The au pair looked at me with her lips pursed, as if she'd bitten a lemon. "Hello, Greta. Nice to see you again."

"I thought you left," she said.

"I did." She looked annoyed, but calm. Hopefully, we could keep her calm until Bartlett and the others arrived. There was a wild look in Greta's eyes that I didn't trust. "I had to come back to get my—" I looked around for an excuse, my eyes settling on Rob's cell phone which rested where I'd left it, on the dining room table next to his scissors. "—My phone. Damn thing. I'm always forgetting it somewhere."

"You'd forget your head if it wasn't tied on," Rob replied.

While we were speaking, I slipped over the threshold and into the house and Rob shut the door behind me. The three of us were standing in the space between the dining room table and one of Rob's counters. Out of the corner of my eye, I could see the knife block sitting near the sink and my mouth ran dry.

"Why are you using the back door?" Greta asked. "You do not live in this neighborhood."

"No, no I don't," I replied, searching for another excuse. "I...um...I knew Rob was in this part of the house, so I came around rather than ring the front door. I hope I didn't interrupt anything."

"Yes," Greta said.

"Not at all," Rob said, speaking over her. "Greta was

telling me about her parents. Interesting fact. Her father was a member of RU Ready. In fact, she says it's me."

"It *is* you," Greta insisted. "My mother told me."

"I was just telling her that it's impossible. There's no way I can be her father."

"That's not true. You are! My mother told me all about you. How you read her poetry and told her she was the most beautiful girl you ever saw. You told her she was special." Her eyes took on an irrational sheen. "You picked her over all the other girls."

Rob shook his head. "I didn't."

"Yes, you did! I even have the bracelet you gave her. See?" The pale blue beads clicked as she held out her shaking arm. Clear pale blue, like the color of water. "She said they matched your eyes."

"Certainly does," I lied. "No mistaking the resemblance." Rob opened his mouth to protest, but I cut him with a warning look. Arguing the point would only aggravate her. Better we keep her talking and get some answers. "You have his eyes too, but I bet your mother already told you."

"All the time," Greta said. "Ever since I was a little girl, whenever I went to visit her, she would tell me the story and say how much I looked like you."

"Visit?" Rob and I asked at the same time.

"*Ja.* At the hospital. She gets sad and confused sometimes." Lifting her gaze, Greta beamed in Rob's direction. "But she never stopped waiting for you to return."

"You must have been thrilled when you realized your new job was only a street away," I said.

"The first time you walked into the house, you smiled at me. I was so flustered that I knocked over a glass of milk. Mrs. Fitzgerald was upset, but you said, 'We don't cry over spilled milk in America.' Do you remember?" Rob nodded. "I remember thinking you were so kind. Exactly how I wanted my father to be."

"You mean, you didn't know Rob was your father when you met? Hadn't your mom shown you photographs?" Or a CD cover?"

Greta shook her head. "My grandmother threw away everything, except this bracelet. Mama hid it, so Oma wouldn't find it. Oma said RU Ready was evil trash."

"Little harsh," Rob said under his breath.

"I knew she was wrong. Just like when Mr. Fitzgerald told me who you were, I knew you were my father."

"Because he's such a nice guy," I said.

"You were everything my mother described. You even teach poetry! How could you not be my father?"

"Greta, I'm flattered, but there's no—" Rob stopped when I glared at him.

"My mother is going to be so happy that I found you. We can be a family again." She threw herself into Rob's arms. Rob looked at me in panic. I gestured for him to put his arms around her, the way a father would a child.

"She never stopped waiting for you," the au pair said, her cheek pressed tightly against his chest. "She wrote you letters."

"I-I didn't know. I didn't get any letters," Rob stuttered.

"People wanted to keep you apart. Horrible people like my grandmother. As soon as I met you, I knew that you would never have abandoned us if you knew."

Where was Bartlett? He should have arrived by now. How long did it take to drive around the damn corner?

"You won't let her keep us apart, will you?" Greta said.

"Her?"

"Diane's selling the house," I told him. "She's letting Greta go."

Greta's face, the half I could see, twisted into a scowl. "Evil witch. Always yelling at me. I hope she chokes."

My angle wasn't good enough to be certain, but I thought I saw a headlight reflection through the window. *Finally.*

"Is that what happened with Alex?" I asked. "Was he trying to keep you apart, too?"

"I thought he was my friend. But he lied. He said he was going to send me away."

"What happened?" I thought of what we'd found in her closet. The scarf and mittens. "Did he find you here when he came by Saturday night?" Then, taking a stab in the dark—no pun intended—I added, "Did he catch you wearing Rob's gloves and scarf?"

Rob dropped his arms from around her and stepped away. "You were wearing me clothes?"

"Don't be upset, Rob. She couldn't help herself. It's the scent, isn't it?" I said to her. "No one smells quite like your dad."

A watery smile crossed her face. Would have been touching, had her eyes not retained their maniacal gleam. "Like coffee and sunshine."

"I know. We found the baseball shirt you keep under your pillow."

"Bloody hell," Rob whispered.

I kept prodding. "It was an accident, wasn't it? You didn't mean to stab him."

"He was supposed to be with Mrs. Rothstein! I came to clean up. To be helpful. What was that?" She whirled around.

"I didn't hear anything," I said. It was Bartlett, opening the front door. "Mr. Fitzgerald got angry when he saw you, didn't he?"

Greta's face started to crumple. "He told lies about you

and said something was wrong with me. He called me 'delusional' and that I couldn't be near his children. I couldn't let him send me away. I just found you."

"So, you killed him," Rob said.

"I didn't mean to! I was upset. The knife was on the counter. I grabbed it and…"

Her tear-stained face looked at Rob, beseeching him to understand. "I never meant for you to be blamed. I tried to put suspicion on Mrs. Fitzgerald. She deserved it."

"And when that didn't work, you tried to put suspicion on Mrs. Rothstein, by telling us about her affair with Diane."

"She never should have yelled at me. I was only trying to help! She told Mrs. Fitzgerald that she should fire me because I was incompetent and disloyal." Her face went vacant as she recounted what happened. "I went to talk to her, to make her take back what she said, but she wouldn't listen. I couldn't let her say those things to Mrs. Fitzgerald. I had to make her be quiet."

She reached for Rob, but he kept his distance. "You understand, don't you, Papa? I did it for us. Because we're a family."

Rob shook his head. A mixture of anger and pity shimmered in his eyes. "No, Greta, we're not a family and you're not my daughter. You're a murderer who belongs in jail." He turned away.

"No!" The denial tore out of Greta's lungs in a loud guttural cry. Before I could move, she snatched the scissors off the table and lunged toward Rob.

34

EVERYTHING HAPPENED AT ONCE. Bartlett burst around the corner, gun drawn. At the same time, I sprang forward, knocking Greta to the ground just as the scissors scraped across Rob's shoulder. The two of us hit the ground, knocking the scissors from her grasp. Bartlett kicked them out of reach before leveling his gun. "Don't move," he said.

I looked up from where I lay splayed across Greta's puffy coat. "Took you long enough."

"Didn't want to interrupt the story," he said. "Besides, you looked like you had things well in hand, until the end." With the gun still on Greta, he held out his free hand to help me up.

That's when I realized he hadn't entered alone. Several uniformed officers'd swarmed the kitchen at the same time. One of them was my son, who was kneeling by Rob.

I scrambled over to join them. "It doesn't look super deep, Uncle Rob," Tim said as he studied the four-inch gash on Rob's shoulder. "I'm going to call in an ambulance to be on the safe side. You might need a stitch or two."

A stitch or two sounded like soft-pedaling to me, given the blood seeping into the yarn, but I kept my mouth shut. Rob looked pale enough.

"This was a brand-new sweater, too, dammit. You owe me a cashmere pullover, Bartlett!" He tried to look over his shoulder at the detective as he spoke, only to wince and straighten his head. Then, grabbing my hand, he kissed my knuckles. "And I owe you, luv. All the cashmere sweaters you want."

Who needed cashmere? All I cared about was that my best friend was going to be all right. "That's all right," I said before kissing his hand in return. "I'll settle for the action figure."

———

SOMETHING BROKE in Greta when she hit the ground. There was a defeated expression on her face when Bartlett pulled her to her feet. She had looked at Rob with a wobbly smile before holding out her arms to be hand-cuffed. Her bracelet caught the light. "Papa?" she'd whispered.

I pushed up my sleeve to show her my bracelet. "Wrong color, wrong guy. Oh, and your eyes? They don't look a thing like Rob's."

"And I dislike Plath," Rob added.

Now, with Greta led away, I stood next to his dining room table and watched as an EMT helped Rob ease onto the stretcher. His silver hair looked familiar. A fellow Fantasy League member, I think. I'd seen him talking to Rob before. Whoever it was, his care was exceedingly tender. Or maybe the emotion of the evening was playing with my imagination. As the EMT buckled the seatbelt, Rob offered a wan smile.

"You planning to ride with him to the hospital?" Bartlett's gravelly voice washed over me like a worn, wool blanket.

I watched the EMT pat Rob on the arm. "I'll meet him there. He looks to be in good hands for the ride. This whole ordeal is going to stick with him for a while."

"Fortunately, he's got an incredibly good friend to see him through." Bartlett handed me a mug that smelled like French roast. "I broke into Rob's secret stash. You looked like you could use a stiff drink."

"I think we have different definitions of stiff." Nevertheless, I took the mug and inhaled. Heaven.

"This version will keep you awake at the hospital."

"Excuse me, sir?" Our conversation was interrupted by a petite female officer. "I was told to ask if you were heading to the Fitzgerald house," she said.

"Tell them I'll be there as soon as I can. I've got things to wrap up here," Bartlett told her.

I took a good look at the officer before she walked away. The woman had hair pulled back tight and soft brown eyes that reminded me of a baby deer. *Cute as a button* was the term that came to mind. My eyes dropped to her name badge. *Hobbs.*

This was Officer Hobbs? I glanced in Tim's direction. His eyes were locked on her like a laser. *Oh Timmy, thou doth protest way too much, don't you?*

Once Hobbs departed, Bartlett's attention returned to me. "Are you sure you're all right? You hit the ground pretty hard when you tackled her."

"I'm fine," I told him. Except for maybe the way his concern made me feel all squishy. "At least this time I got a confession without drinking any drugged tea. I'm improving."

"That you are." Then, in a completely out-of-character

move, he tucked a hair behind my ear. "You make a decent detective, Ms. McIntyre. Even if I do have to run in and save your ass at the end."

He slipped the coffee mug from my fingers and helped himself to a long sip. From across the rim, I could see his eyes sparkling. He was flirting, dammit. At a crime scene, no less.

I took my cup from him. "Just for that," I said, "I won't tell you how capable you look with a gun."

"I already know."

Okay, now he was just being cocky. Unable to help myself, I smiled as I drank.

Cocky or not, he was damn impressive when he burst around the corner. The kind of virile white knight they write books about. A girl could get used to having a guy like that hanging around. In more ways than one.

"Thank you," I said.

"For what?"

"Being so reliable. For riding to my rescue. Again."

The corners of his mouth melted into a smile. "Anytime."

Our eyes locked and for a moment we were the only people in the room. My mouth suddenly ran dry. I think it was caused by the blood rushing upward to my ears. When had he moved so close? All I had to do was stand on my tiptoes and we'd be a breath away from kissing.

What was one little kiss? A peck of gratitude if you will. I brushed my lips against his. He tasted like coffee, mint, and Bartlett. There was no other way to describe it. We looked at each other and smiled.

"Hey, Mom! Do you need a ride to the hospital?"

Mid-twenties and my child still interrupted romantic moments. Any residual guilt I had about walking loudly into rooms when his high school girlfriends were visiting disappeared. "Thanks, but I'll drive myself."

"Are you sure? You've been through a lot."

"I'm sure, honey."

My answer must have reassured him, because he immediately folded his arms and mimicked a stern, parental stance, "I'm glad, but honestly, Mom, you've got to stop playing amateur detective. One of these days you're going to get yourself in real trouble."

"Exactly what I was saying," Bartlett replied as he sauntered away. Just before leaving the room, he turned to catch my eye.

And winked.

35

A WEEK LATER, I was pulling into my driveway when my phone rang. I smiled when I saw the caller ID.

"Congratulations," Bartlett said when I answered. "A certain patrol officer told me that his mother sold the Rothstein house before it even hit the market."

"What can I say? Theresa loved the place. Apparently, she and 'Christopher' loved the idea of someone being murdered in their kitchen."

Plus, no one ran on Poplar Street. No one did much of anything anymore. Diane stayed true to her word and moved back to her parents the day after Greta's arrest. Stu Rothstein put his house on the market not long after. Neither he nor his daughter wanted to stay in their house a moment longer. I am not proud to say that I called Theresa immediately, but a commission is a commission. Renee said she was proud of me, then passed me a list of obituaries and suggested I make cold calls. I threw out the list.

"And how was your week?" I asked him. "I saw on the news that Greta was arraigned."

"She was, and she pled guilty. All that's left is wait for the sentencing hearing."

"Thank goodness. It'll be nice to return to normal. Hopefully, the judge will assign her some anger management classes while she's in prison."

Her temper was Greta's downfall. Well, that and her obsession with Rob, although considering she spent her childhood being told fairytales about RU Ready, the obsession part was somewhat understandable. Losing her temper and striking people? Different story.

Once Bartlett put her in handcuffs, Greta told him everything. Most we already know, but she filled in the rest of the blanks. Turned out she'd been letting herself in and out of Rob's house for weeks, collecting mementos and making herself "useful." The day we found her cuddling Eliot? He hadn't escaped. She'd brought him outside so that when Rob returned home, she could win points for the rescue (along with helpfully steering the investigation toward Tonya).

Poor Tonya. Her death had nothing to do with the murder after all. All she did was suggest her friend get a better au pair. Her recommendation earned her a cast-iron skillet to the back of the head.

Alex's death played out much like we suspected. Greta had returned to Rob's house after the party where she helped herself to the snowman's accessories, replacing the mittens with her own. There were no footprints because she entered and exited through the front door. Meanwhile, what few footprints she didn't make in the yard blended with the rest of the party traffic.

"The one thing we never did figure out was where Alex was heading when he died," I said to Bartlett. "We suspect he stabbed the snowman as a warning to Rob, but nothing explains why he didn't go to the closest house."

"I have a theory about that. The Rothsteins live across the street from his house. I think Alex was attempting to head home to his kids."

"Makes as much sense as anything else. Alex adored his kids," I said. "And he had just discovered his au pair was unstable."

"Exactly. As a father, his first instinct could have been to protect his kids. He wasn't thinking about what he would do once he got there."

"Considering how badly he was bleeding, I suppose we should be grateful he showed as much logical thought as he did. If he hadn't stabbed that snowman, we might still be running around in circles."

"We?" I could tell he was arching his brows on the other end of the line.

"Fine. You," I said. "Satisfied?"

His chuckle floated through the line. "With you? Always? And you can stick with *we*. I like the sound of it."

Damn, he made me weak-kneed when said those kinds of things, and he knew it, too. The bastard. I tried to form a witty comeback, but my brain wasn't working quickly enough. He was speaking again before I had a chance to open my mouth.

"How is our favorite British professor doing?" he asked. "I hear he's making morning appearances at Cuppa Joe's."

"He is, and he was welcomed back with a hero's welcome. Jenn told him the band wasn't the same without our head gorilla."

The day after Greta's arrest, Rob and I kicked down the snowman. (I kicked; Rob watched, thanks to his stitches.) When my foot smashed the final chunk of snow, I caught him wiping his cheek.

"He's doing the best he can," I added. "I think he's still processing everything. Oh, he did call Benjamin Twitmire and let him know he might have a daughter." Greta's bracelet was Twitty's collectible color.

"Bet that was a fun call."

"It was for Rob." That earned a second chuckle. "I'd better let you go," I said. "You're probably busy with non-murder investigations."

"Actually…" He dragged out the word. "I called for another reason. I've decided it's time I look at living in something more permanent than a rental. You wouldn't happen to know a good real estate agent, do you? One that won't hesitate to throw herself at a killer if things get rough?"

"I might," I said with a smile. "Why don't you come by the office tomorrow and I'll show you some listings?"

"Can't tomorrow. My day's all tied up with, you know, crime things. How about we meet in about an hour? I could describe what I'm looking for and you can send me a list of suggestions?"

I looked at my watch. An hour would make it dinner-time. "Well, I was going to microwave some leftovers," I said, "but I could push my plans until later."

"Gilroy's has a dinner-for-two special. It's a Valentine's Day special, but there's no reason we can't take advantage of the deal, too, right?"

No reason besides some destroyed police evidence. On the other hand, I did have that new little black dress wasting away in my closet. And Gilroy's holiday specials were a great deal….

What the heck? It was only dinner, right? Dinner and, if I got lucky, another kiss. Only a fool would turn down that opportunity.

My mama didn't raise no fool. "I'll see you in an hour."

Happy Valentine's Day to me.

THE END

ABOUT THE AUTHOR

Barbara Wallace is the author of over two dozen romance and mystery novels. Since her debut with Harlequin Books in 2009, she has sold nearly 1 million books internationally, including in the UK, France, Greece, and Australia. She and her husband of 31 years have one son - who recently added a wife to the family. They currently live in New England with two cats that get way more attention than they deserve.

You can contact Barb through her website at www. barbaratannerwallace.com. While there, please take the time to sign up for the Barb Wallace Bulletin so you'll be the first to know when the next Sadie McIntyre book is available. Also, don't forget to follow Barb on Book bub.com for recommendations and info about upcoming releases.

ACKNOWLEDGMENTS

For those of you who read *The Suburbs Have Secrets*, you know that this book was originally scheduled for Spring 2018. Well, you know what they say about best laid plans. The last two and a half years have been a wild ride, to say the least. There were two deaths (three if you count the cat), a wedding, a major family move, a retirement, several other contracted books that pushed this book down the queue, and finally, a pandemic. Thank you for your patience.

There are two poems quoted in this book. "Pippa Passes" by Robert Browning, and "Song" by T.S. Eliot. Both poems are in the public domain. I'd hoped to have Rob quote one of Eliot's cat poems (since that seemed appropriate), but alas, they have been copyrighted. Thanks *Cats*!

And now, a few thank you's….

Thank you to my BARWA Sisterwives, Donna, Shirley, Renee and Jenna, as well as my text buddies, Penny and Lesley. The six of them listened to me stress out for two and a half years. Their patience and encouragement was invaluable.

Special thanks to my content editor, Mary-Theresa Hussey of Good Stories, Well Told. She, too, had a crazy two years, and yet she managed to find time to help me make this story the best it could be. Thank you as well to Words Between Pages Editorial Services for their copyediting and proofreading services. Without them, who knows what gobbledygook you would be reading.

Also thank you to Selena Blake of Ecila Media for creating such terrific covers.

Lastly, thank you for reading. The Sadie McIntyre Mysteries are a labor of love for me. To know there are people who enjoy them as much as I do, makes me very grateful.

THE SUBURBS HAVE SECRETS

Gossip Can Be Deadly

BARBARA WALLACE

A SADIE MCINTYRE MYSTERY

When Sadie McIntyre gives a drunken Marylou Paretsky a ride home on a rainy night, little does she realize it's the last time anyone will see Marylou alive. The following morning, Marylou is found dead at the bottom of her staircase, the victim of foul play.

Who killed Marylou? Was it her philandering husband? His lover? Or one of the residents Marylou was blackmailing? In a town where everyone has a secret, the list of suspects is endless. To make matters worse, Sadie is hiding her own secret. One that, if discovered, could shoot her to the top of the list!

Can Sadie find Marylou's killer before her secret becomes public? Or will the killer find her first?

1

Everyone has secrets.

Take, for example, the good folk of Woodbridge, Massachusetts, population 7,256.

Like many of the leafy suburbs outside of Boston, Woodbridge has beautiful, tree-lined streets and acres of manicured community athletic fields. It's the kind of town that routinely places high on those Best Places to Live lists.

And it's just bursting with secrets.

Trust me, I know. Having sold real estate in Woodbridge for the past nine years, I can safely say I've seen more dirty laundry than most. Just this past week, for example, my client opened what she thought was a utility closet in the basement and found the seller's dominatrix supplies. Needless to say, the riding crop collection discouraged them from making an offer.

That's the thing about secrets. Eventually, they get out. And when they do…

The fallout can be murder.

―――

2

It was half past seven, Sunday night. I was on my way home from a wildly unsuccessful open house and debating whether or not I wanted to drown my sorrows in a bottle of Riesling when wham! Out of nowhere, a dark figure stepped in front of my car.

I slammed on the brakes. Thankfully, I wasn't driving fast, so I screeched to a halt inches shy of a collision. The person—whoever it was—didn't notice. Head down, the figure crossed the street…

And promptly crumpled to the ground.

I got out of my car and hurried around the hood, stopping short when I reached the left headlight. The person sat cross-legged in the middle of the road, face obscured by a dark navy hood. "Are you all right?"

The person muttered a reply. From where I stood, it sounded like "stupid street."

I stepped closer. Probably not the best idea, seeing as how I was alone and dealing with a potentially crazy person. Then again, curiosity has always been my downfall.

"Hello?" I said, reaching for their shoulder. "Do you need some help?"

"Don't touch me!" "the person screeched, and jerked away from my touch. In the process, they fell backward, knocking the hood away.

"Marylou?"

"Stupid street. "Freaking tilted off balance."

It was Marylou Paretsky.

At least she had Marylou's voice and pudgy face. The Marylou I knew wore pastel twin sets and chirped her words like an excited chipmunk. The woman in front of me looked like a street person. Her navy-blue sweatshirt was two sizes too small. I could see her stomach protruding out from beneath the hem. And her hair, normally neat as a pin, hung in a half-done ponytail, the sandy brown curls flopping in her face. When she turned, I caught raccoon circles of mascara lining her eyes.

I watched as she struggled to stand up, only to get her feet halfway under her body before sitting again. "Stupid street. Stop moving," she muttered.

She was drunk as a skunk. "Here, let me help you up."

"Leave me alone. I'm fine." The protest might have had more oomph if she hadn't tipped over trying to slap my hand away. Not even trying to save herself, she fell and lay with her cheek smushed into the blacktop. "'M perfectly fine."

"We weren't going to get anywhere this way. Grabbing her upper arm—this time she was too busy lying down to wave me off—I tugged her into a sitting position.

"Stop it! Gotta stay here. Gonna listen to me."

Listen? If she kept hollering in the middle of the street, the whole neighborhood was going to hear her. I looked around at the houses with their curtains drawn. Thankfully, we were on the north side of town where the houses were set farther back from the sidewalks. Plus, everyone would be settling in to watch the eight o'clock game.

"You can't stay here," I told her. "We're in the middle of the street." Dear Lord, but she reeked. Alcohol. Mothballs. There was a third smell in there too I couldn't identify. It might have been sweat. "Tell you what. Let's get you home, and you can sit there."

"No! Gotta stay. It's impo-portant."

Impotent or important? I didn't get to ask because she managed to yank free of my grip and crawled on all fours toward the curb. Dignity was clearly off the table at this point.

At least we were out of the street though. We were making progress.

That's when she threw up.